A City Imagined

A City Imagined

Edited and introduced
by
Stephen Watson

PENGUIN BOOKS

Published By the Penguin Group
Penguin Books (South Africa) (Pty) Ltd, 24 Sturdee Avenue, Rosebank,
Johannesburg 2196, South Africa
Penguin Books Ltd, 80 Strand, London WC2R 0RL, England
Penguin Group (USA) Inc, 375 Hudson Street, New York, New York 10014,
USA
Penguin Group (Canada), 90 Eglinton Avenue East, Suite 700, Toronto,
Ontario, M4P 2Y3, Canada (a division of Pearson Penguin Canada Inc.)
Penguin Ireland, 25 St Stephen's Green, Dublin 2, Ireland (a division of
Penguin Books Ltd)
Penguin Group (Australia), 250 Camberwell Road, Camberwell, Victoria
3124, Australia (a division of Pearson Australia Group Pty Ltd)
Penguin Books India Pvt Ltd, 11 Community Centre, Panchsheel Park,
New Delhi – 110 017, India
Penguin Group (NZ), Cnr Rosedale and Airborne Roads, Albany, Auckland
1310, New Zealand (a division of Pearson New Zealand Ltd)

Penguin Books (South Africa) (Pty) Ltd, Registered Offices:
24 Sturdee Avenue, Rosebank, Johannesburg 2196, South Africa

www.penguinbooks.co.za

First published by Penguin Books (South Africa) (Pty) Ltd 2006

ISBN-13: 978-0-143-02473-6
ISBN-10: 0-143-02473-6

Typeset by CJH Design in 10.5/13.5 pt Charter
Cover photograph: Dale Yudelman
Cover design: Flame Design, Cape Town
Printed and bound by CTP Book Printers, Cape Town

Acknowledgements

I would like to acknowledge the support of the Cape Tercentenary Foundation and especially that of the National Arts Council in making the publication of this book possible.

A special thank you is also owed to Dale Yudelman for his willingness to allow us to reproduce the photograph on the cover of this book; to Sean Christie and Jane Rogers for their invaluable help in the preparation of the manuscript; and above all to Tanya Wilson for her support throughout.

Contents

Introduction

I

The idea that has prompted this book, as is doubtless the case with many another, lies in a certain sense of deprivation. Though books on Cape Town abound, ranging from guides to its flora to studies of local architecture, local flu epidemics not excepted, there has been none to date that has addressed itself to the particular spirit of the place, the *genius loci* that is inalienably Cape Town's own and like no other on this planet.

As a much younger person, born and bred in this city, I was aware of this lack, finding few reflections of Cape Town in the literature and artwork that I happened upon. Although this was more the result of my own ignorance than the place's fault – there was indeed a literature in and of this city, some of very long standing – much of it that I proceeded to read left me empty-handed or otherwise unappeased. Either it failed to match my sense of the place, or else it seemed not equal to the challenge of representing it. Whether it was Rudyard Kipling or other, locally born writers, the evocations of the place were, for the most part, notably thin. Ironically, there seemed a more resonant echo of my city in the essays of Albert Camus, writing of his native Algiers – 'a city open to the sky like a mouth or like a wound' – and especially calling to mind his memory of the summers of his youth spent there: 'What you can love in Algiers is what everybody lives off: the sea visible from every corner, a certain weight of sunlight, the beauty of the race.'

Nevertheless, that Cape Town was and is a remarkable city, whether in its own weight of sunlight or street-corner glimpses of harbour and sea; that it possessed a combination of qualities like no other, worthy of any of the forms of literary or artistic pursuit – this was always self-evident to me. Hence this book. I have asked a number of writers, some very well known, some less so, the majority of them current citizens of this city, to write a personal essay in which they attempt to take the measure of the place and to define its meaning for them.

Long before writers like DH Lawrence brought the notion into prominence, the conviction that every place harbours a particular spirit has been common enough. But Lawrence was also alluding to something which, no matter where in the world one might pursue it, is rather like one of those rare birds that, indubitably in existence, is not at all easy to see clearly, let alone capture. Accordingly, I have given the writers gathered here carte blanche to come at Cape Town in any way that might best suit their individual pursuit of it. Although some have chosen to focus on a particular district of the city, this was not a requirement. They were all of them free to adapt the essay form – that often underrated yet infinitely malleable form – as they deemed necessary. I did not want a collection which would come across as a formally identical set of responses to one set question. Above all, I wanted a book the quality of whose writing – whatever the individual sensibilities and angles of vision at work – might come close to this city and the qualities that are uniquely its own. That seemed, at the very least, its due.

Every writer's consciousness may be likened to some custom-built prism through which light from a common source will be differently absorbed and refracted. What one of them might notice may well remain below the horizon of another's attention; the sea whose immensity may be a life-long passion for the former may well be the pretext only for an immense boredom in the latter. But the place of one's life *is* one's life and no writer can avoid configuring (and reconfiguring) that place both in the light of consciously held aesthetic ideals and also in line with the deepest tendencies in his or her nature. No person can look at a landscape, and no less a city and its environs, without making these over, however subtly, into his or her own subjective terms.

One of the pleasures of this collection, I hope, will be found in seeing how each writer, defining his or her relation to Cape Town, also defines himself or herself. But the refractions gathered together here are necessarily many – and all the more so, given the contemporary moment. In the past it has been common to hear that Cape Town comprises a tale of two cities only. There is the city of the privileged, their rose and vanilla mansions hugging those contours of privilege close to the city's mountain chain, its forest slopes, and better beaches. On the other hand, there sprawls the immense city of the dispossessed and deprived, the apartheid dormitory towns and squatter camps, steadily filling up the waste ground between the city's mountain backbone and the barrier range of the Hottentots Holland.

So staggering is the distance between the extremes of wealth and poverty in this city, so dramatic the abyss dug by these extremes, that one might be forgiven for believing this tale of two cities to be the only truth about the place. But even half a century ago, in 1959, when the writer Anthony Delius disposed of Cape Town in half a line – 'old age home of liberals and culture' – his idea of the city as a place both obsolescent and moribund, a kind of death genteelly warmed over, was no more the whole truth about the place than the reproach, still lazily recycled, that Cape Town remains Little Europe incarnate, ie not really an African city.

Of course it's not an African city; it's much more complex, and interesting, than that blanketing term permits. (For one thing, it's always been a coloured, or Creole, city.) In any case, the greater truth must be obvious to all by now: Cape Town in the last ten years or so has been undergoing the greatest period of change in its entire history. Globalisation, that process that permits so few exceptions to its rule, has lately entered this city with consequences for its life, good or ill, still largely unforeseen.* At the same time the flood of economic migrants from the rest of South Africa, as well as the influx of refugees from places like Angola, Burundi and the Democratic Republic of Congo, continues unabated, bringing with it a weight of needs whose consequences are similarly incalculable.

But all these people, rich or near destitute, have brought with them other languages, cultures, religions, skills, multiplying the human realities of this city, altering the character of some of its districts as never before. Although the present life of the city's three million or so inhabitants does not yet license the near cosmic conclusion that Peter Ackroyd reaches at the end of his massive *London: The Biography* (2000) – 'London goes beyond any boundary or convention. It contains every wish or word ever spoken, every

---

*Cape Town, one now reads, is the second most popular place on the planet for UK residents to own a second home. Today there are city estate agents who do business, and doubtless good business, selling off segments of its coastline, site unseen, to foreign investors.

4

action or gesture ever made, every harsh or noble sentiment ever expressed. It is illimitable' – there is a sense in which Cape Town is now an entity about which one knows only that it can never be known – or never in its entirety. Not one of the old myths of this city seems halfway adequate to its present realities. Lawrence Green's vision of Cape Town as 'the tavern of the seas' has belonged, long since, to a bygone era; it did not really survive the construction of the new container harbour or the refurbishment of the Waterfront (manifestly a tripper's, not a sailor's, paradise). The same could be said of any of the other mythologies of this city, whether they hark back to the myth of that presiding god, Adamastor, or to that ambiguously maternal figure of the Mother City herself.

In fact, there is no longer any single, dominant myth about Cape Town for the simple reason that this city has lately changed, expanded, diversified to such a degree that no one myth could any longer contain it. Its ways are many, its realities multiple, often contradictory when not wildly incongruent. To each claim that this one or other feature stands as the essence of the place, there might be a dozen counter-claims, each equally valid. Here, no less than others elsewhere, Capetonians live in a profuse world. Given this, it seems no happy coincidence that the essays included in this book, whatever the common ground they travel, reveal a tale not of two cities, but of nineteen. Had the number of contributors been greater, then I'm certain that the latter figure would have increased accordingly.

II

Cities of whatever stamp are no more separable from writers and the idea of writing than they are from the idea of civilisation itself (originally, to be civilised meant to belong to a city, to be a citizen). Great cities, in particular, are virtually synonymous with great writers; commonly, it is the latters' words and works that have been crucial in establishing the status of the former. If Dickens had not written his novels, London, no matter what its expansion since, would be a diminished place. If Cavafy had not, in his poems, re-envisioned Alexandria as a city of learning and sensuality, its lustre would have all but sunk beneath the present-day squalor of the Egyptian city. Paris is the echoing, endlessly resonant city that it is because one cannot walk the streets of that metropolis, even today, without certain lines of Baudelaire coming back to one. The same could be said of Florence, shaped by Dante's bitter-sweet vision of it, or the Buenos Aires re-cast by the young Jorge Luis Borges in terms of that passion that he signalled in the title of his first book, *Fervor de Buenos Aires*.

For writers, as for others, it is no less true that cities are also the most seductive spaces probably ever created. Not only do they promise financial rewards, they have the generic allure of all places alight in the dark. Unlike the monoculture of the village, they give many things, among them the promise of pleasures both complex and varied. Emporia of possibility, cities have always presented not only a vision of one's own life, but of other lives, possibilities without number. They are, in this respect, the ultimate in psychic poultices: they draw us forth. They enlarge the scope of what we thought life could be – or was always fated to be. They inflame longing even when what they promise might be rudely withheld or never fulfilled. No wonder, then, that historically the most common relationship that holds between a writer and a city is the one defined by any great object of desire: namely, that of the romance.

If this is true of Scott Fitzgerald and New York (and

as it would be, later, of Woody Allen and his relationship with Manhattan), then it must be said that Cape Town, though lavish in its ambience for lovers, is not a particularly romantic city. While it has continued to be the literary capital of South Africa, the city itself appears to have remained a more obscure, rather than explicit, object of its writers' desires. Or the romance its presence has elicited has evidently never been particularly strong.

Nor has it held much attractive power for Americans and disaffected others, seeking a corner of the world in which to expatriate themselves. Though some novelists, like Mary Renault, once lived here for years, this city was never Tangiers; it has never had its Paul Bowles. Baudelaire, one assumes, must have stepped ashore at Table Bay, en route to Madagascar in his delinquent youth; but there is no record of this. Late in life, TS Eliot, his lungs unable to withstand another London winter, holidayed at the Cape. But there is, likewise, almost no account of his impressions. Often enough literary travellers have been no more effusive than the Greek poet, George Seferis, on a brief visit to Cape Town in 1941: 'Nice place. Dull people' – such were the two phrases he committed to his diary.

The reasons for this paucity are not hard to find. Cape Town, like all other South African cities, has long had to carry the burden of all cities of colonial origin, sometimes years after their founding. This is a life marked and marred by a culture much of whose weight has been lost in its translation from its parent culture. For centuries almost everything in the city's history conspired to produce a condition akin to the one that Albert Camus, writing of his native Algiers again, was at pains to note: 'Between this sky and the faces looking up to it there is virtually nothing on which to hang a mythology, a literature, an ethic or a religion – only stones, flesh, stars and those truths the hands can touch.'

This cultural degree zero (for that is the condition Camus is referring to) may have been mitigated in Cape Town in all sorts of ways. But it is undeniable that there was long a species of vacancy about the place, an underbelly of melancholy to it, no matter how copiously and cheerfully sunlight might pour down upon it. This was in fact a cultural vacancy that went hand in hand with a spatial vacancy – the colonial city that has not yet managed, through architecture, to tame and humanise the space around it; and which, still existing like some permanently unfinished building, works to infect all space around it with its incompleteness, its emptiness. And part of this lay in the fact that much of its life lacked significant representation in art or literature.

The obstacles to this were doubtless always formidable. No less than the painters in Australia's colonial period, who persisted in representing gum trees as elm trees, it was manifestly impossible for writers in earlier periods here to see the Cape other than through colonial eyes. Moreover, their responses were often muted, not to say overwhelmed, by the sheer size, the presence, of the landscape which they had come to inhabit. (Writing of the immense skies of Arizona, JB Priestley gave similar grounds for the relative dearth of writing in that state: 'No real poetry has come out of Arizona, and not much painting. Nature is doing it all.') And then Cape Town, a city haunted by its own clichés more than most, particularly its spectacular confluence of buildings with mountain and sea and sky, has always possessed the kind of beauty that tends to embarrass intellectuals and writers – physical beauty being the sort of thing that cannot easily be intellectualised, let alone tamed.

If we are now a long way from that colonial city, it remains true that Cape Town persists as a place not much mythologised by its writers. Even now, when its citizens and tourists go to the beach here, they step into water, colder or warmer, but not into literature. If they should venture as far as Muizenberg, they will be entering a wind-corroded seaside suburb, not an ethos, let alone a mythos. In Cape Town, to this day, beach culture takes effortless precedence over book culture. And doubtless many Capetonians, as well as visitors, would affirm that, given the physical assets of the place, this is the precisely natural and right order of things.

III

But this is also – a word of warning, perhaps – not how things are in this book. Which is to say, the reader of these essays will find in them more incidental than central reference to many of those scenes and sites that have made Cape Town one of the planet's premier tourist attractions – 'a world city', as the brochures now like to bill it. No Parisienne loves Paris primarily because of the Eiffel Tower, landmark and wonder though it may be. No Capetonian, I would venture, really sees the Waterfront as central to his or her idea of the place, even though some might give one reason to suspect otherwise.

The reader will, however, discover something here which, though less commercially valuable in its benefits or prospects, is no less indispensable to the life of a city and its citizens. This is the record of the ways in which a number of writers have inhabited Cape Town, and how this city, in its turn, has come to inhabit them – ie has taken up residence in their inner world – often at the deepest level. This is the place formed by the entanglements of reality and imagination, the meeting of inner and outer weathers. As with any city that has been truly lived in, loved, and at times suffered, it is a space coloured by memory, ambivalences, disaffections, obsessions. But this is what is meant by a city *imagined* – the title of this book. Such is the place, after all, where most of us live, whether we are writers or not.

While I was putting together these pages, Henry James's famous argument for the necessity of literature kept coming back to me. 'It is art that *makes* life, makes interest, makes importance', he wrote, urging for this reason that there was no substitute for it. No less implicit in his argument was the conviction that it is art, and the art of writing more specifically, that also, crucially, makes for the interest and importance of place. For the world's great cities are great because, apart from embodying depths in time that not even archaeology can sometimes fathom, they are spaces which have been greatly imagined by their writers, even in their deprivations. While they remain as material as the stone and brick from which they've been built, they resonate for their inhabitants and visitors according to the shapes that various imaginations have found in them, as well as the structures that these minds have erected upon them. Without such, whatever their other eminences or prominences, all cities would remain so much real estate – or, alternatively, landfill.

In this connection it strikes me, more and more, that there is a kind of miracle that attaches to all creative work, large or small, and which is no less miraculous for being commonplace. It is to be found in those many instances in which human beings, impelled in one or other way, have taken it upon themselves to bring something into existence – such that there, where once there was nothing, or next to nothing, there is now something. It may be no more than an image, one poem perhaps, something far less than a book. But each serves – this being the miracle – as a kind of reflection which, though it could never offer a perfect or complete mirroring of ourselves or our world, nevertheless works to deepen the surface of that world, to thicken the textures of its reality, adding depth to its resonance and thus substance to our lives. Writers, as will be seen from those gathered here, all know this. They know, too, that this is why we cannot desist from imagining, and re-imagining, the place of our lives.

Stephen Watson

Damon Galgut

My Version of Home

You ask me to tell you about Cape Town. But although I would like to talk about it with detachment, with an objective and knowledgeable distance, I find I can't. For me, that detachment, that distance, would be fake. My life is so bound up with this city that any separation from it is impossible. All I can give you is my limited and loaded perspective: my own version of Cape Town. Which is made mostly of ignorance.

*

I have lived here for nineteen years – almost half my life – but it still doesn't quite feel like home. One is always somehow just on the verge of belonging. No doubt my nature is partly to blame. But it seems to me there is something in the nature of Cape Town too – something that accepts and refuses, attracts and repels – which makes this state of ambivalence almost inevitable.

Set up, quite literally, as a refuelling station, a halfway point between other destinations, the notion of transience was built into it from the beginning. From the earliest colonial days, people were always passing through. Criminals and riff-raff from Europe, poor immigrants in search of a new life, slaves imported from the East for labour: much of the population came from somewhere else, torn out of the past and trying to forge a future. It started life as a frontier town.

And in many ways it is not so very different today. Of course it isn't a refuelling station any more; it has long since become a destination in its own right. Like every other South African city, Cape Town is changing fast. But it is changing, perhaps, in distinctive and revealing ways. Whole blocks are being ripped down to make way for glossy new apartments and offices; huge areas of the city bristle with building cranes; money jingles loudly on the air. All of it smells of property, progress, cash and greed: something new for a place that, until just a decade ago, still used to feel like a small town.

This kind of rapid, heady development is a magnet for people in search of a better life or a fast buck, and they have come pouring in, bringing with them their own little charge of restlessness, of transience. Immigrants and refugees, con men and entrepreneurs: part of the local population is always in flux, always passing through. So some of the volatility, the sense of impermanence, from the old days has lasted. A touch of the frontier has remained. It is still a place where different cultures push against each other, sometimes violently. And there is, to a degree, the same atmosphere of lawlessness. We like to present our clean and civilised face to the world, but a big portion of the local economy is driven by crime. Gangs, prostitution, smuggling, drugs, corruption

– the real frontier, continually being rolled back, is the limit of what's possible. Fate and fortune shaped by human will: it is a vision of power bequeathed to us by empire; and it continues to draw hungry, greedy, visionary people from all over the world, coming to try their luck.

So my own sense of being a visitor, an outsider, is perhaps not that unusual. Even less so when you consider another kind of visitor the city has become host to in the last ten years: the tourist. Indeed, insofar as it thinks of itself at all, Cape Town thinks of itself as a tourist city. That is, a city which gives pleasure to people who are, by definition, passing through. And the pleasures that it offers are not those of 'history' or 'culture', but in a certain sense their opposite: what it offers is beauty.

The idea of beauty – ephemeral, abstract – has always been connected with Cape Town. Even the accounts of the first white settlers, though heavily laced with fear of wild animals and the threat of the unknown, make repeated mention of the grandeur of the setting. Some of those early enthusings are not very different from the postcards that modern visitors send home. And even those of us who live here reach easily for those terms: 'I come from Cape Town,' we might say. 'Such a beautiful city!'

By this we tend to mean not the city itself, but the natural backdrop of sea and sky and mountain. Above all, the mountain: it features over and over, in reports from three centuries ago to the most recent magazine articles. There are very few cities in the world with a mountain at the heart of them. It is the mountain that makes Cape Town recognisable, that gives it its particular distinction. The other elements of the landscape – the rocks, the vegetation, the colour of the sea – might be rare in a city too, but they do at least conjure other possible places. The Mediterranean coast, for one, often comes to mind. But it's the unmistakable

14

graph drawn by the triptych of Devil's Peak and Lion's Head, with that imposing flat-lined plateau between them, that lets us know exactly where we are.

Which is why most photographs and pictures of Cape Town like to use the mountain as an anchor. It is the real skyline of the city. Most of these pictures are idealised: soft-focus shots across the bay from Blouberg beach, high aerial portraits, twilight takes of the glimmering streetlights against that definitive silhouette.

In many ways the mountain is Cape Town's most permanent feature; everything else is in a state of flux and flow. Not even the sea has stayed where it was. Beginning as a straggle of fortified buildings, the city is now a vast sprawl that covers half the peninsula. Under this kind of siege, it is a testament to the enduring power of the mountain that it continues to overshadow the most prodigious efforts to subdue it.

Permanence in the midst of transience: yet the mountain is more than that. It embodies, also, a symbolic force that – depending on the weather – either looms threateningly or hovers luminously over the human lives below it. What makes Cape Town extraordinary – perhaps the *only* thing that does so – is the brooding, absolving presence of Mother Nature Herself.

Try to picture the city without it. So intimately have the mountain, the water, the sky, been grafted onto our lives that it's almost impossible to imagine what would be left over if the natural world were removed. But the profane truth is that most of Cape Town – the physical place of streets and buildings and bridges – is not, actually, very beautiful. Some of it is downright ugly. Poor planning has cut us off from the sea. Unfinished highways dangle eternally in space. When bad weather descends, certain streets wear their melancholy like a grey hat pulled down low over the eyes. Squalor and

15

poverty are inescapable; indeed, they constitute the lives of most of the city's inhabitants. But even in the most expensive, upmarket areas, misjudgement and bad taste abound. There are, yes, little picturesque pockets here and there, small touches of architectural grace, but they hardly redeem the overall impression, which would be far from uplifting if the city were stripped of its dramatic and vivifying setting.

Of course the setting is real. The mountain is a genuine presence. But rather than the airbrushed view across the water, it is more likely to be foregrounded in a scene of mud and shacks, or the entrance to a shopping mall. The forest hovers greenly overhead, but nearer at hand is a stretch of road flanked by second-hand furniture shops and laundromats and pizza parlours. The blue waters of the bay call to us, but first we must cross the parking lot in the wind, under the shadow of the sports stadium.

If there is an essential quality to Cape Town, it doesn't lie in either its beauty or its tackiness, but in the tension between the two. There is always a promise, and then a denial of that promise. Some floating dreamy vista draws the eye, while a more powerful gravity weighs down the feet. A transcendence seems to be offered, while the human reality is anything but transcendent. This conflict, this push-pull of the eye and heart, is what keeps one forever on the threshold, about to step through the door.

The natural world, of course, is not physically out of reach. This is one of Cape Town's greatest pleasures. One can lie on the beach, or climb the mountain, or walk in the forest. At such times it is the city that recedes into the background; one seems to have arrived at the dreamy destination. But does one ever arrive? The point about beauty is that it excites yearning, but you can never, ultimately, hold it in your hand. So part of being in Cape Town is made of longing, a kind of spiritual hunger that is never satisfied.

But there is more to it than that. It seems to me – and maybe only to me – that, even at its most unspoiled, there is something cold in Cape Town's loveliness. It doesn't have the sensual pull of the tropics, with their promise of decadence, or the tawny violence of an essentially African landscape. The sea is too harsh for languid abandon. The fynbos and low scrub give a feeling of nakedness and exposure; both the earth and any human action seem bared to the cleansing glare of the sky. This is beauty, yes, but not a beauty that heats you up into action, that throws you outward into the world. The effect, rather, is the opposite: of introspection and inwardness. The extremes of climate – especially the wind and rain – fold the spirit in on itself. The impulse is towards asceticism, to contemplation and meditation, not in the direction of sensual interaction. The spectacle of nature, everywhere in evidence, draws you towards it, but at the same time, paradoxically, into yourself.

There are occasions when this paradox does provide moments of near-epiphany. There are times – and this evening, as I write, is one of them – when a particular conjunction of light and water creates a point of crystalline stillness, both in the world and in yourself. Table Bay is flat and utterly calm, broken only by the anomalous shapes of an oil rig and a small boat, reflecting a sky empty except for an unmoving bank of cloud. It is a picture painted in shades of grey, with a quality of reflected light at the heart of it that is almost painfully pure.

Such moments are authentically part of the city too, and reason enough to live here. But they are exceptional, and part of their power is religious. That is to say, they remind us of eternal, timeless qualities, which will outlast us, and in which we have no part. Which is why Cape Town's beauty often evokes a feeling of melancholy isolation in the observer, made deeper by the transience of those epiphanic moments:

already the light is fading on the water, the ordinary world is starting to return ...

So one is here, but not entirely present. Something is nearly always withheld. And that incompleteness, that sense of a gap between the world and yourself, is what one comes to associate most deeply with Cape Town.

*

It is a condition that has penetrated into the very idea of ourselves. Most great cities in the world become imprinted on the people who live in them, in the form of particular qualities and attitudes. We know what is meant by 'a typical New Yorker', for example, or 'a Parisian intellectual'. But the term 'Capetonian' is slippery and imprecise. At most – and tellingly – it evokes the idea of somebody vague and hedonistic. A stoned surfer type, perhaps, or maybe a mountaineer. In any event, a dreamer: somebody distracted from the real business of the world. Somebody not entirely present.

On a subliminal level that distraction, that absence, may be true of all of us who live here. But in everyday life, the real Capetonian character is far more complex and contradictory. Most of us, in fact, aren't dreamers at all. It's a relatively small and well-heeled portion of the population that can afford to spend its time doing tantric meditation or cantering around on horseback, behaving like an actor in a cigarette advert. That notion of Cape Town – of idle contemplation or vigorous outdoor activity – is a tourist fantasy, part of the promise of transcendence. The negative print of the fantasy is a scene that Cape Town readily offers too: a lonely, broken, homeless figure, stumbling through the rain. On one hand, exaltation; on the other, degradation.

Most of us live somewhere between those two extremes.

But that's as far as any generalisation will go. For the rest, and for obvious historical reasons, our communities and cultures are so divided that we come, it sometimes seems, from different places. There is no centre, no common core, to which we all belong. And this, too, becomes a kind of exclusion.

Anybody who doubts this should take a walk through the centre of town. The few blocks around the Castle are where the city first sprang into life and they are still the truest indicator of what it means to live here. The station or the taxi rank, the Golden Acre and the Grand Parade, Long Street and the Company Gardens – these points stake out one of very few, relatively tiny areas where all the various populations of Cape Town mix together, rub up against each other, before retreating again to their far-flung neighbourhoods. It's no accident that a part of the city where people, as yet, haven't set up permanent home should be a showcase for all of Cape Town's different communities. They are there in transit, for work or socialising, only passing through.

The faces you will see here, in this part of town, are a glimpse of how various and complicated and separate the lives of the city are. You will see humour and ingenuity and wit, and occasional instances of a spectacular hybrid beauty. But you will also see the face of the psychopath flashing past like a blade. There are the over-tanned rich sipping cappuccinos at outdoor cafés, jewellery clinking in the breeze. And there are many, many lives pitted against mediocrity or poverty or bad odds, or even just the weather, for whom victory is less likely to come in a cathartic moment than in the slow business of enduring.

These different spirits and histories do not add up. In the end your own face is just one more in the crowd: another element in the dissonant harmony. And while you search in vain for a single story to unite all these characters, you may experience again that sensation of transience, of restless not-quite-belonging, which may be the only unifying story we have.

Damon Galgut was born in 1963 in Pretoria. He has published five books, the latest of which, *The Good Doctor*, was shortlisted for the Man Booker Prize, the Commonwealth Writers' Prize and the IMPAC Dublin Award. He lives in Cape Town.

Finuala Dowling

Spring and Neap

I slow down for you on the scenic drive, change into first gear while your behemoth tour bus mounts the wide pavement above Bailey's grave. I don't mind the delay. I love this view too – though 'love' doesn't explain the way the local coastline has franked me, left a watermark in my heart, moulded its own relief into the soft grey matter of my cerebellum.

What has the tour guide told you? Perhaps he has explained why the shallow bowl of blue behind you, as you pose now for a photograph, is called False Bay. Perhaps he's pointed out that there are true bays within it, providing safe wintering for ships and perennial mooring for boats.

He probably hasn't told you that the entire population of the world could be stacked uncomfortably into its basin, like a messy heap of washing up. My environmentalist brother finds this thought consoling, which is why I offer it to you.

Your guide may have mentioned that in a nearby kloof

grow pristine yellow-woods, and, on the mountainside above you, flourishes an erica that can be found nowhere else in the world. Erica, Erica, I know how you feel.

This route via Boyes Drive is worn through with the heart-full homecomings of my forty-three years. When I am away from here, my closest emotional relative is the outcast male baboon, the one you might have spotted a moment ago, perched on a fence post overlooking the vlei, his hair backlit by the sun. From the outside he may appear to be picking his fleas in debonair fashion, but inside, I know, he feels sickened and adrift.

I think I should pull over, come stand beside you as you survey the nursery sets of Surfer's Corner, the beach stretching east, east, east as if it would like to disappear into the very rays of sunrise. I should let my eyes move slowly with yours to Koeëlbaai, Rooiels, Hangklip, then across to Miller's Point. There is a restaurant there where the waiter, pointing with his tongs at the proffered tray, names the different kinds of wet, raw seafood the chef could cook for you today. I hope you are not thinking of lunch already.

We could instead walk a little way along the low stone wall towards Kalk Bay, where I live, and look down on the curved arm of the harbour. 'Curved arm' – that reminds me, for years I wanted to write about this place, but couldn't because the first sentence of every juvenile effort of mine contained the word 'nestled'. To hell with this, if I can't describe Kalk Bay without launching straight into journalistic cliché, let me desist, leave you to take home that classic, serene shot of sea, boats, bathing boxes.

Or would you let me try to make the picture postcard come to life? Ask me anything. Look down over the narrow main road, lined with millionaire houses (the poorer cottages wedged behind and between), look beyond the railway line to the rocky coast and ask: 'What's that? What's that?'

22

That is the St James tidal pool, and that tiny dot standing on the wall is a poet of my acquaintance. The subtly changing speck on the sand is a man performing his t'ai chi exercises, and walking briskly past him on the catwalk is my sister. (She is upset because the sign there has been erroneously translated into Xhosa as: 'There is no alcohol here.')

Or, looking right, that is Dalebrook pool, and the little figure on the rocks, being stretched forward by his two red setters, is a retired Shakespearean actor who will stop off at Quagga Trading for a chat and a browse on his way home. I turn to see if this is making any sense to you.

I know that wistful look. I too have caught glimpses, in foreign cities, of natives stepping inside private doors, disappearing down clandestine alleyways towards unimaginable pleasures. I've stood outside, staring at the hard surfaces of famous buildings and statues, aflame with curiosity about the seven dimensions that my foreignness denies me. Your guide has named things for you, but you do not know our names.

I offer to take you home in my rusty, un-air-conditioned, sandy-floored, loose-ceilinged, happily rattling Cape Town car. The transcendent view is all very well, but to know this place you must step off the dais and walk its narrow, sometimes cobbled streets. You must steep yourself three hundred and sixty-five days in its heady brine.

Come, live with me. This is what you will find – spring and neap, catastrophe and slow, long resurgence.

In summer, we wake to the engines of the fishing boats at four, or earlier still, to the slam of a neighbouring fisherman's door. *These Foolish Things* is the tune he's humming. Drift off again or accept that it's time to get up and write before a morning swim.

Hennie the bergie, smelling of wine and urine, is sitting in the dew-damp park when we take our short cut past the wooden jungle gym. He tells you he was once a hygiene inspector. With all due respect, this is hard to believe.

Hennie is famous for falling into a drunken stupor next to the tracks and losing his fingers to the morning train. When he knocks, we put money in the whole hand and hang a plastic bag of food or empties over the stump. When they die, the Kalk Bay bergies get notices in the obituary column and a well-attended funeral at Holy Trinity.

It's only just after seven as we descend to the subway under the railway line. There, another homeless man still sleeps on his cardboard. (If it is election time, you will see a politician's eye peeping up at you.)

We put our towels on the rock shelf, duck in quickly and swim our lengths with a solitary heron or cormorant for company. Even leopard sharks find their way in on occasion.

Beyond the tidal wall, the sea ripples and leaps into life, briefly elucidating that difficult line about Antony: *his delights/Were dolphin-like; they show'd his back above/The element they lived in*. A pity my second-year students aren't here. A pair of less literary kayaks glides by. Other swimmers join us now: it is rush hour at Dalebrook.

Something unreal is happening too. Among the rock pools, a thin model is posing for a film crew. This is utter crap: no one twists her torso in one direction and her head in another, her pretty skirt trailing in a rock pool, at quarter past seven in the morning.

On our way home, the village coffee shops are open for business; the who's who of Cape Town (no, not us) are ordering cappuccino. Until Olympia renovated its bakery space, hot croissants came down Windsor Road from the old garage on a tray. (I have slowed down for croissants, too.)

No leisurely breakfast for we who only live here. We work all day in our home offices. My brother built my study for me in our back yard. The wall on the mountain side has an agricultural drain in it somewhere, and about three different structural layers. It had to be signed off by an engineer. That's how heavily the Silvermine Reserve leans against me.

It may look like a bohemian life, but it's not all pure art. The painter in Rosmead Road builds film sets; the better-known local authors make their real living out of journalism and education; I teach sometimes but right now I'm writing a guide called *English for Science Students*. Says a witty friend: 'No wonder there's an educational crisis in this country when they get poets to compile maths text books.' It'll be the only science guide in the world illustrated with Gus Ferguson cartoons. ('Do you have any books on chaos? No, but we have some on order.')

In the balmy evening, we lie on recliners in the garden, behind a hedge dripping with hibiscus, and drink gin or wine. Everyone assembles: family, friends, children, dogs and kittens. Live jazz drifts up from the Brass Bell, with a slight delay on it like an international phone call.

My youngest brother talks about past life therapy and his latest message from the dead. Perhaps this is what inspires my daughter to describe the school camp. On the School in the Wilds farm, she tells us, there is the grave of a man who reputedly hated children. Angelique, the thinnest girl in the class, her hair in a tight bobble on top of her head, leapt gleefully onto his tomb with her spindly legs and chanted: 'I'm alive and you're not! I'm alive and you're not!' Such sweet revenge.

A plate of biscuits with leftover cheese is passed around. If someone has had forethought, there will be ciabatta or calamari.

The Hottentots Holland turn purple and the sky goes pink over the silver-blue sea. Somebody sheltering in a nearby bush is smoking such a mound of marijuana that we also become mirthful. It's true that there's a tree on Trappieskop behind Peggy's house, near the fishermen's flats, with a hand-made sign saying 'Dagga for sale here.'

Stay another day. Stay many days. Stay for the night of the pounding sea.

In the roaring dark, mad rollers hit the breakwater, shooting up walls of water before crashing over the pier. Our bay windows are filmed over. Waves chuck seaweed and sand onto the concrete pathways at the beach, flood the sub-ways and create a huge bath of Omo in Dalebrook.

After the storm our morning swim is crazy. The subway is knee-deep in dodgy-looking flood water, so we hop over the railway line, leaving our towels up against the rail-way embankment. In the teeth-crackingly cold water and wildness, it's impossible to tell where the pool ends and the ocean begins. Foam fills our mouths and eyes, and we laugh out loud.

On the reef, schoolboys are surfing six-foot waves. Their mothers wait impatiently in cars, one eye on the clock. There will be some very late, cold and damp boys at Fish Hoek High's assembly this morning.

All through December, January, February, we swim. It's better when the water temperature drops because then our brief immersion will keep us cool through the inferno heat of the day. The thick walls of my tall old house also shut out the sun. But the garden is desiccated. For months the plants have had nothing but the occasional salt spray or dousing of dirty water. We ourselves shower only briefly, surrounded by buckets. I no longer make jokes about the thousand-litre rain tank my brother gave me for Christmas.

Day after day of relentless thirty-degree heat, only tempered by high southeaster winds. They too are a liability. Soon a single careless cigarette butt will set off the fires of summer.

A character of mine once joked that 'Cape Town is always on fire, it has something to do with the sex life of the fynbos'. In truth these fires are eerie, bringing fears of personal incineration. At Fish Hoek corner, after a particularly destructive blaze, I swam among blackened fragments of an unknown family's photographs.

I was six years old when the first home I knew burnt down to its three-hundred-year-old foundations. Cinders blowing across Boyes Drive ignited the resinous alien trees around the old homestead. My parents were out – father riding, mother playing golf. Family retainers clambered onto the thatch with pots of water. Neighbours bustled in to carry out the furniture. 'Quickly, quickly, choose, choose what you want to keep.' I looked in my cupboard: there was nothing there that I wanted above any other thing. Only every beam and floorboard. Later the *Cape Times* showed my father among the debris throwing open his hands in capitulation. Father of eight says he is homeless. Perhaps it was too dramatic – someone offered to adopt us.

At last it happens: a whiff of smoke, the crackle of dried vegetation surrendering to the flames. Within twelve minutes from call-out, helicopters strafe the ridges and gulleys. On the reef, surfers laugh nervously and remonstrate. But the pilots, choosing their three thousand litres nearby, only seem to tease them. The giant red Bambi bucket is dragged overhead; its light spattering of water feels like a benediction.

Night falls, but the mountain behind us is alight. Sleep is fitful under a single sheet. A brother, volunteering to fight the fire, is nearly trapped between two walls of flame. Pushes the bakkie through, makes it.

Now sirens close in from all directions. Ash is settling in the garden; the air is acrid. We switch on Cape Talk and listen to the Eyewitness News, volume loud against the whirring blades. Light reflected off their metal creates occasional flashes across our windowpanes. Houses are being evacuated.

We're on national television. Cape Town's helicopter crews have flown their maximum number of hours: they must rest now. The camera gives a shot of pilots from Water-kloof airbase filing onto a troop carrier to relieve their shattered colleagues.

When we think we can bear it no longer, it is over. The wind dies down. A mist rolls in from the sea; drizzle dampens the last smoking embers.

We attend art exhibitions and poetry readings, think about joining the film society or a Latin American dance class at the community centre, or Helen's philosophy group that meets at Habanero's.

Everyone is suddenly well. A local mother who had turned reclusive comes out again, walking a new puppy. A vagrant on a rehabilitation programme run by the night shelter is rumoured to paint like Cézanne. It's been six months since someone last stole one of my tyres. Hennie tells us, apropos nothing, that he believes he's still fertile. We try to look pleased.

We continue to swim until the end of May, when it turns cold and rainy. These houses were designed for summer; many were in fact boarded up in the cold season. So in winter we huddle next to log fires, clutch hot-water bottles, dig out threadbare pairs of long johns. We run out of kindling. I use my daughter's broken dolly furniture and the melted remains of my mystical brother's meditation candles.

Now we walk on Fish Hoek beach in the mornings. A thin sliver of moon the night before means that the next day's sand is flat, hard, inviting. Along the grimy tide line, baby box jellyfish gleam like costume jewellery. At the corner, among the hardy winter swimmers, a romance is blossoming between the man with a public-school accent and the woman with the prettiest bathing cap. We pretend to be watching the trek fishermen.

One day our beach walk is interrupted midway by a police officer who asks us to turn around because there is a dead body up ahead, 'and it's a bit early for that kind of thing,' she says. So there is a suitable time in the morning for the viewing of washed-up corpses.

The next day Ossie the dentist and his friend who seems to be unofficially in charge of the beach (the way he plants his thermos on his bonnet and surveys the scene), tell us that the dead body was of a young woman, her wetsuit unzipped and breasts exposed. A mermaid we suppose.

Three suicides in Fish Hoek in just this fortnight alone. A Zimbabwean pensioner shot himself in the avenues. I wonder whether it was the same old man I saw looking longingly at the turkeys in Shoprite's chest freezer in December. He took a packet of pet's mince.

The *Argus* headline asks, 'What the hell is going on?' I used to think it was the job of newspapers to answer that question.

The rains come and our allergies turn into full-blown colds. The storm water drains are blocked with a year's worth of debris and litter; there is nowhere for the runoff to go when the water table rises. Mountain streams burst their banks, the fire-depleted soil becomes a mudslide; Boyes Drive is closed to traffic.

In between torrential downpours, we clamber up the old stone steps and take an evening walk in the cool, damp air. The road has a reclaimed look. Mud and leaves partly cover the tar; the absence of traffic and people takes us eerily back in time.

I point out the large car park in the village below. There was a school there once, open to all. The other parking area, near Olympia, was where the wagons outspanned. I know this because of the tiny private museum on Ponder Steps. Miss Moss of Moss Cottage keeps every single newspaper cutting about Kalk Bay; she has documented every historical reference, collected every black and white photograph. (Her husband builds model railways – they run through the house.)

There were cows here once, a dairy, and the long house beyond Theresa's restaurant was a hospital. The local fishing families used to drag harpooned whales up the beach. There must be whale bones buried beneath that old white house opposite the harbour traffic lights, the one with the deep stoep and blue shutters that has seen so much.

The whales still come in spring, undeterred by what our ancestors did to them. My mother complains that they interrupt her conversations: at any moment her interlocutors will exclaim at the wondrous spouting, breaching, blowing, hooting discernible from our front windows, and she loses her thread.

We climb up Waterfall Steps to the contour path, let the wet flowers brush our faces on the overgrown paths. A girl I knew was raped up here when we were seventeen. Trapped, she told her little sisters to run. Later, one of the detectives on the case introduced her to horses; they became a lifelong love of hers. She married a kind man.

Downhill is easy, we're soon at the road again. A short walk and we find your tour bus waiting. You'd better climb aboard. Here, don't forget your camera.

Finuala Dowling is a freelance writer, lecturer, editor and materials developer. She has published two volumes of poetry, I Flying and Doo-Wop Girls of the Universe, as well as a novel, What Poets Need. Her short stories appear in local and international anthologies. She lives in Kalk Bay.

Michiel Heyns

On Graciousness and Convenience: Cape Cottaging 1960–c1980

When I first came to Cape Town, as a callow but in certain respects precocious schoolboy, the city prided itself on its *graciousness*, which meant that it had no night life and that everything closed at one o'clock on a Saturday – other than the cinemas, which had a three o'clock matinee, and, as highlight of the week, an evening performance to which people wore suits (if male) and stoles (if female). On Sunday, by law, absolutely nothing happened.

Graciousness, I came to see, was a peculiarly English quality, and Cape Town was a peculiarly English city: for all the forlorn reminders of another heritage, the Buitengracht, the Heerengracht, the Buitenkant and the Waterkant, its main street was Adderley Street, and the shops were named for their owners or founders, who clearly were English:

Stuttafords, Garlicks, Fletcher & Cartwright's, Darters. Even physically Cape Town resembled an English city.

Seeing London for the first time in 1970, I was struck with how *familiar* it seemed: the Victorian buildings, the shopfronts, the stations. And, of course, the Public Conveniences. Apart from the cavernous piss-palaces under Leicester Square and Piccadilly Circus, almost every tube station and many street corners sported a solidly built, well-maintained Convenience – or cottage, as it was known to those who cottaged.

The Oxford English Dictionary cites the earliest usage of *cottage* as a verb – *To use or frequent public toilets for homosexual sex* – as 1972, but by that time it was well overdue. Joe Orton's diaries, written from January 1967 to his death in August 1968, could serve as a guide to the public toilets of the London of the time, and clearly Orton's appropriation of them required a verb, and a strong one at that. With the esotericism of the connoisseur, Orton favoured 'a little pissoir – just four pissers' on Holloway Road, whose hospitality far exceeded its proportions, accommodating, on one occasion, eight men in intimate conjunction: 'the little pissoir under the bridge had become the scene of a frenzied homosexual saturnalia. No more than two feet away the citizens of Holloway moved about their ordinary business'.

As in London, so (more or less) in Cape Town. The old station, tragically demolished in 1964 to make way for the no-place that is the Golden Acre, was a town within the city: a pub, shops, a restaurant – and a Public Convenience of noble proportions. I would say there were at least thirty individual porcelain urinals, arranged in two rows that faced each other, or that would have faced each other had the planners not considerately built a wall between, so that one had, in effect, two long narrow rooms, both lined with a row of stalls, both accessible by a door at either end. One of these rooms also housed a row of cubicles.

The design provided space and opportunity for a certain amount of circulation and selection. It was not uncommon for someone to walk in, survey the incumbents of one row, and then disappear around the corner to the other. If, after some seconds, he returned, he had evidently not found there the more desirable option he had envisaged. Those he had originally spurned were now not inclined to be accommodating, unless he was so irresistible that all pride and principle withered under his gaze.

The place was a temple to the unconsummated marriage of scopophilia and exhibitionism: those not content with the you-can-look-but-better-not-touch ethos had to go elsewhere to follow up a likely prospect, which the convenient location of the old station in the city centre simplified. In the immediate vicinity were several lesser but convenient cottages, the closest of which was in the OK Bazaars. The place lacked *je ne sais quoi*, but it was ... well, convenient.

I was too young then to register such distinctions, but I now suspect that the OK Bazaars would have been regarded as not quite the place to be seen. More discriminating shoppers went to Stuttafords across the way, which had more extensive, cleaner and more active Public Conveniences. These were located on the same floor as the Books department, indeed adjacent to it, which provided a respectable and educational excuse for loitering.

The Stuttafords cottages were a bastion of discretion: the entrance was screened from public view by a passageway-partition, an architectural hybrid of a modesty board and an air lock, allowing an inconspicuous, not to say surreptitious, re-entry into the public arena, very convenient for those customers making more frequent entrances and exits than mere nature could plausibly dictate.

The Stuttafords cottages could not compete with the

station in terms of scale or conception: their forte was al-together graciousness, and even, within the constraints of their function, elegance. I remember an understated beige-pastel interior, with a spacious antechamber lined with a veritable archipelago of handbasins. I never counted, but I suppose there was one handbasin for every pisser, on the assumption that a gentleman would no more share a handbasin than a pisser. Here there was always much wash-ing of hands, drying of hands, combing of hair and peering into mirrors, as preliminary, intermediate, advanced or exhausted stages of negotiations in the inner chambers.

The first of the inner chambers contained the pissers, the centrepiece of any true cottage. These, though, after the magnificence of the handbasins, were a let-down: only two short rows of stalls, no porcelain niches, only little protruding slabs of masonry to protect the modesty of the incumbent and stay the hand of the contiguous. The rows were back to back, running counter to the very essence of cottaging, indeed of all cruising, which is eye contact; here the over-the-shoulder exchange of glances was likely to lead to nothing more exciting than a crick in the neck.

Perhaps because of these drawbacks, Stuttafords was less celebrated for its pissers than its cubicles, which extended beyond the stalls, in a single row of about eight, with a narrow corridor in front. Privacy was not absolute, in that the walls between cubicles did not extend to the floor, allowing the more adventurous Stuttafords shoppers to communicate with occupants of adjacent cubicles, in ways limited only by the ingenuity and suppleness of the par-ticipants. On a good day, which tended to be a Saturday morning, all eight cubicles could be occupied for long periods. The blatant and the desperate queued up outside, trying to appear oblivious to the rustling, shuffling, scuffling and scrambling sounds emanating from the cubicles. It was bad form to catch anybody's eye in acknowledgement of a particularly expressive sound, though on one occasion everybody laughed when a muffled '*Eina!*' was heard. It was not done to greet anyone emerging from a cubicle by name.

On the way out, inside the door, was a mirror at what would have been euphemistically called waist height, with a discreet little sign saying '*Gentlemen are requested to adjust their clothing before leaving.*'

For some cottagers the Stuttafords conveniences were too public for comfort, and, having established an understanding of common purpose, they sought tranquillity elsewhere, one party following the other at a discreet but visible distance. This was as perilous as carrying an egg in a spoon over broken ground: one party could change his mind for no apparent reason, or bump into a loquacious acquaintance. No such mishap intervening, one could make it to a safe haven such as the Syfrets Building on Greenmarket Square, which offered unhindered access to its well-appointed cottages on each landing, its cubicles fully enclosed, with tight-fitting doors.

The only drawback of this accommodating building was that the terrace of the Inn on the Square overlooked the entrance, and anybody with half an eye for body language could spot a successful pursuit on its way to resolution. I once, while having a toasted sandwich on the terrace, saw a friend, whom I shall call Schalk, then recently married, come sauntering up, followed at a discreet but unmistakable distance by a young man similarly sauntering. Schalk, with a quick backward glance, disappeared into the Syfrets Building, and so, very casually, did his pursuer. They emerged, together, about quarter of an hour later, shook hands, and went their separate ways. The point of sex in public places, I suppose, is that it is public, at times more public than one realises.

Zackie Achmat's laconic, forthright account of his boyhood, *My Childhood as an Adult-Molester*, wittily describes his delighted discovery that the Observatory station toilet, which he first visited because he wasn't allowed to use the library toilet, was frequented by white men who cared as little as he for the racial barrier: 'Apartheid forced me to use Observatory Station toilets, but apartheid was destroyed in those toilets. By men who had sex with men, regardless of race or class.'

It is tempting to hymn the cottages as centres of subversion, outposts of resistance to patriarchy (and I don't doubt that Zackie shook up the preconceptions of quite a few pillars of the community), but I suspect they mainly affirmed the conventions they offended against. The cottage is the public face of the closet: Gay Pride it's not.

A different way of dignifying cottaging might be to see the cottager as a *flâneur*, whom Edmund White describes in his *The Flâneur: A Stroll through the Paradoxes of Paris* (2001) as 'that aimless stroller who loses himself in the crowd, who has no destination and goes wherever caprice or curiosity directs his or her steps'. White appropriates the term to his own more particular application of it: 'To be gay and cruise is perhaps an extension of the *flâneur's* very essence, or at least its most successful application.' He is unrepentant about what would seem to have been a singularly successful career: 'Of course, most people, straight and gay, think that cruising is pathetic and sordid – but for me, at least, some of my happiest moments have been spent making love to a stranger beside dark, swiftly moving water below a glowing city.'

Well yes. But White's swiftly moving water is the Seine, his glowing city is Paris, and he was meeting his strangers in the shadow of Notre-Dame. Even Stuttafords didn't quite match up to that.

The Cape Town that revealed itself to me was, I suppose, queered by my perspective on it. But no city has a single identity, and Cape Town was also a community of cottages with its own band of secret citizens. However little overt solidarity there was amongst this disparate group, they shared a language of signs, of gesture and glance, and they traced their routes and established their landmarks over the official map. They had no loyalty each to each: at the merest hint of a police presence they could drop whatever they had in hand and disperse in a spirit of *sauve qui peut*. But it was an understanding of sorts, a ritualised interaction with strangers that mocked the graciousness of white South Africa. As Joe Orton knew, every cottage potentially hosted a saturnalia.

And today? I simply don't know, having retired from the field some years ago: there can be few activities on earth, other than break-dancing, less congenial to the over-forty than cottaging. But if it is true that cottaging thrives on repression, then there must be much less of it: there is now the Gay Village, Steamers or the Hot House, Virgin Active, Sliver or the Bronx, or, failing all these, the Internet, where like can meet like without inconveniencing others or being inconvenienced. We must not lament, I suppose, the passing of cottaging.

Postscript, 6 June 2005

It strikes me that I need not speculate about the fate of the cottages of yore: they are, after all, visitable, or the sites are, where once they mutely ministered to their errant flock.

I park in the Golden Acre; I calculate that I am close to the spot, five floors down, where my train would have pulled in when this was still the old station, and thus not far from where the Public Conveniences dispensed their hospitality.

The arcades are full, bustling, noisy. There are many institutions offering quick loans. The main commodity on sale seems to be fast food: chicken in every possible ethnic packaging, burgers and doughnuts, schwarmas and samoosas, nuts, sweets and fruit; cold drinks and coffee, meat pies and muffins. Signs warn that *'This is a no-smoking area.'* The toilets have massive turnstiles like a soccer stadium and charge fifty cents per entry, a flagrant violation of the basic principle of cottaging, which is the free circulation of trade.

Where the OK Bazaars used to be there is now a Shoprite. I enter: inside, everything is different, but finding the Parliament Street exit, I recognise the staircase that used to lead up to the mezzanine, and the rather grand lift lobby. The mezzanine has disappeared; a dead wall conceals the bare ruined choirs where late the sweet birds sang.

I make my way to the station. There is a rail strike on, and the place is relatively quiet, though once again a cornucopia of food stalls fills the spaces where once there were ... well, spaces. A sign proclaims *'This is a no-smoking area.'* The Convenience close to the mainline station is still there: here, after the demolition of the old station, the scattered tribe for some time half-heartedly congregated, hoping to re-establish the old faith in an alien territory.

The large U-shaped urinorium is much as it was, except that the mirrors at each corner, which facilitated surreptitious glances, have disappeared. There are not many people at the stalls, and a practised glance establishes that most of them are on legitimate business. There is only one loiterer: he has an unlit cigarette in his mouth and is glancing around nervously, as if considering whether it is safe to light up. I wonder if it is an offence to loiter with intent to smoke.

I have my pee; there is relief in not feeling obliged or tempted to linger. On the way out I check the cubicles.

Several of them lack doors, some lack toilets. The Public have absconded with the Conveniences.

Outside in the sunshine, where once there was an open space abutting the rather sterile gardens, there are now hundreds of stalls selling running shoes and handbags. Cape Town, or this part of it, is no longer gracious. It is a working city filled with working people and dedicated to their needs and tastes. Edmund White says: 'The *flâneur* is by definition endowed with enormous leisure, someone who can take off a morning or afternoon for undirected ambling.' Central Cape Town is no place for the *flâneur*.

It is lunch time. I am not attracted to Nando's or Chicken Licken, and I wander up Long Street looking for something more – well, I suppose, gracious. I chance upon Caroline's Cape Kitchen, which promises oxtail. I enter. Only three tables are occupied. At one, on his own, by one of those co-incidences that in fiction would seem far-fetched, is Schalk. He beckons me over and invites me to share his bottle of Sancerre. In honour of the wine I order Cape yellowtail.

'What are you doing in town?' asks Schalk.

'Research,' I say, and tell him. 'Do you remember Stuttafords?' I ask.

He laughs. 'Of course,' he says. 'The big trick was picking up somebody on the escalator.'

'Oh?' I say. '*Now* you tell me.'

'Yes,' he says. 'You remember, going down you had a view of the people going up and vice versa. Well, the idea was to catch someone's eye going in the opposite direction; the excitement was to see which one would change direction. But it made more sense for the one going up to turn round and follow the other one down and out.'

'Yes,' I say, laughing, 'to the Syfrets Building.' I tell him how I had observed him leading his conquest into the building.

He is amused. 'So we shook hands?' he says. 'It didn't always end so politely, did it?' Then he shakes his head. 'Wonderful,' he says, 'how every building had a toilet on every landing, and you could get in without going through a security check. Security has killed cottaging.'

'Zackie Achmat says he found sex and tenderness in the cottages,' I say. 'Would you say you found *tenderness*?'

Schalk considers. 'I don't know about tenderness,' he says, 'but a sort of solidarity, a sense of having the same shit to deal with. So there was the shared plight, the recognition of an affinity, making contact in the midst of thousands of people who suspected nothing.'

We have another glass of wine each. He tells me he discovered cottaging three months before he got married. Now, twenty-five years later, he is no longer cottaging, and is about to get divorced. I don't know what the moral is, and ask him.

'I don't know either,' he says. 'I can't say cottaging saved my marriage. But it certainly made it tolerable.'

We do not have dessert; Schalk returns to his office and I resume my pilgrimage. I walk around the block that once was Stuttafords. The pavements are as wide as ever, but thronged with stalls selling puzzlingly large piles of vitamins and patent medicines. The large windows, so convenient for checking the whereabouts of a pursuer, now reflect such a jostle of stalls, customers and pedestrians that to pick out one shadowy figure would be impossible. Besides, where would one go with him?

I walk up Shortmarket Street to Greenmarket Square. After the wine I need to pee and there is a cottage on the Square. It always was, and still is, too busy to be cruisy, frequented by stall-holders and customers alike: that rare thing, a Public Convenience that is a convenience to the public.

Where the Inn on the Square used to be, there is now a Famous Butcher's Grill: no doubt better adapted to business lunches than toasted sandwiches on the terrace. Where the Syfrets Building used to be, scaffolding and signs announce some new erection. Only Sturk's Tobacconist remains, a diehard establishment serving the needs of a dying clientele. '*Zware Shag now in stock*' says a handwritten sign in the window. Another system of signs intelligible only to the initiated. Outside Nedbank a young woman and an older woman are standing smoking. They are not talking, merely sharing the same space for a common need. Smokers: perhaps they are the new breed of oppressed, the secret sharers.

I drift towards Church Street, named for the Groote Kerk with its pulpit by Anton Anreith. I still feel, after the fish and the wine, the need for something sweet. The Cafe Mozart is closing, and I continue down Church Street, past the Association of Arts building; on the left is the Café African Image, a small bright interior, tables and chairs and a stuffed pink flamingo outside. The blackboard announces sweet potato and coriander soup and *malvapoeding*. A pleasant young woman, whom I take to be Afrikaans because of the *malvapoeding*, takes my order. I order the soup rather than the pudding, and a glass of white wine.

I survey my surroundings. The building opposite has a restaurant on the first floor with tables on the veranda. Would it still be Bukhara? On the ground floor, where there used to be a bookshop, Clicks destroys the street's pretensions to Afro-chic and to everything else. Across the street from Clicks, where Peter Visser Antiques used to be, is another African curio shop.

My order is brought by a young black man with his dreadlocks in a multicoloured snood. The manager, if that is what she is, sits down at a nearby table and lights a cigarette.

A young white man unlocks a bicycle from a stand nearby, and stops to cadge a cigarette from her. His eyebrows are plucked, and, stereotyping, I guess that he works for the Association of Arts. The woman comments on his bicycle.

'Yes,' he says, 'if I took a taxi it would take me ten minutes to walk to the station, another ten minutes waiting for the taxi to fill up, by which time I could have been in Observatory already on this.' He thanks her for the cigarette, leaves.

A young black woman comes out of the café and joins the manager. She gets up every now and again; she runs a stall selling African knitwear nearby, and helps prospective customers try on her wares.

A grey-haired man walks past, and shouts, in a heavy European – Spanish? – accent at my waiter, 'Hey rasta! You a real rasta yet?'

A middle-aged white man comes to join the manager at her table; then gets up and goes to his stall next to the young woman's knitwear; he sells antique glass and silver. The prospective customer is only looking, and he returns. Pausing at my table, he says, 'Business is not exactly booming.' I think, but don't say, that African knitwear is selling better than antique silver.

He leaves, and I order another glass of wine with my soup, which is very good. The oil cloth on my table has a bald pink saint on it, surrounded by an ornate text: 'Saint Antoine de Padoue, Priez pour Nous.'

I ask the manager about this European touch to her African restaurant. 'Oh no,' she says, 'that's Congolese.'

She tells me that she has worked in Greece and in London and then in the Waterfront; she now feels for the first time that she is actually staying in Africa. I've been taught by the *Mail & Guardian* that Cape Town isn't Africa, and I want to say something self-conscious and insufferable like this isn't exactly Kampala, but fortunately refrain.

I settle down to my second glass of wine. Offices are closing and workers are hurrying past. The wine in the winter afternoon sun is very mellowing, and the vision of Used to Be recedes: I see Rainbow Nations and African Renaissances and Multicultural Communities. When I get to Hybridity I realise I'm drunk. I leave.

On my way back to the Golden Acre I walk through Woolworths, about as gracious as this part of town gets nowadays. I still want something sweet, and I select a packet of wine gums in the food hall and join the not-inconsiderable queue. There are eighteen check-out points but only three cashiers.

The man behind me, an elderly Muslim, complains about this. 'Where are all the cashiers?' he asks. 'There used to be twelve.'

I point to the *Argus* on a stand nearby: '*Strike cripples city*.'

'That's where they are,' I say. 'Probably couldn't get to work.'

'I don't know,' he says, 'what's happening to this place. Nothing's working any more.'

The wine still working, I consider his statement.

'I don't know,' I say. 'I think most things are working fine.'

He looks at me, offended at my failure of shopper solidarity.

'What's working fine?' he demands. '*Woolworths* isn't working fine.' His tone announces the end of civilisation as we know it.

'I don't know,' I say. 'Everything seems so much more … *convenient* than it used to be.'

Michiel Heyns lectured in English at the University of Stellenbosch until 2003, when he took retirement to write full-time. Apart from a book on the nineteenth-century novel and many critical essays, he has published three novels. He lives in darkest suburbia in Somerset West and is at present working on a translation of *Agaat* by Marlene van Niekerk.

Jeremy Cronin

Creole Cape Town

Any attempt at rethinking creolisation in a South African context should state outright that it is not about 'race-mixture' in the sense that the apartheid government would surely have defined it. The ability to undergo creolisation, in other words, is not exclusive to people socio-historically legislated and assumed to be of 'mixed' ancestry.   – Helene Strauss

Trumpets. A roll of drums. And the bare-chested actor steps out proclaiming from the prow of his trireme: 'I ... am ... Ajax!' 'DA FOAMING CLEANSER!!' comes back the response from a hundred choral voices up in the balcony, in tribute to a popular washing powder of the day.

The Criterion bioscope was opposite Jubilee Square and next door to the Rendezvous Café along Simon's Town Main Road. It was here that I learnt two early lessons. The first was a lesson in the popular deconstruction of the imperial (in this case Greco-Hollywood) epic. The second was a related lesson about the possibilities of upending apartheid hierarchies.

Simon's Town's small African community had lived in Luyolo, a precarious camp built up the side of the winding road to Red Hill. In the late 1950s, by the end of the first decade of apartheid, the camp had been destroyed and the families forcibly removed to townships closer to the city. But there was still a sizeable Coloured community living in Simon's Town, and so the Criterion's regular matinee patrons (some of us very regular, watching the same film many times over) were segregated into a 'European' and a 'non-European' section. The upstairs balcony belonged to the 'nons'. It was from there that a continuous subversive choral commentary emanated. It was an exhilarating, part stereophonic, part bipolar disorderly experience. It was hard to tell what was more entertaining, the action on the silver screen, or the flow of interjections from up behind. Both tugged at the heart and imagination.

Before interval, with its lucky ticket-number draws and hula-hoop and yo-yo competitions, there would be a serial. Usually it was a short Western. That is when things would become seriously hectic. It was fine so long as the pioneer settlers with their ox-drawn wagons were suffering a weekly litany of natural woes – buffalo stampedes or prairie fires. It was even tolerable when a whooping line of painted, pigtailed braves ambushed the settlers with a blizzard of arrows. It was the finale that always caused the problem. As the music rose in anticipation, as the United States cavalry flag topped the rise, as the mounted heroes poured down the hillside to rescue kith and kin, those of us, the 'non-nons', down in the ground-level auditorium would know to duck behind our laager of upturned bioscope seats as a torrent of popcorn cartons, apple cores and peach pips rained down in protest upon our 'European' heads.

Cape Town, of which Simon's Town is an outlying suburb,

has long been a contested space. In the post-apartheid era, however, there has been something paradoxical about its status. Cape Town, this beautiful city, this prime tourist attraction, is not generally well liked by many of the new political and professional elite in our country. (I hasten to add that – white as I am – politically, vocationally, objectively I am part of this new elite.)

There are many reasons for the dislike. There is Cape Town's political 'unreliability'. It is the one major city not securely under an overwhelming ANC majority. There is the liberal smugness of its leafy suburbs, secure in the knowledge that the property market will continue to regulate what apartheid administratively held asunder. There is the history of a divide-and-rule, 'Coloured labour preference area' policy. This policy is partly the reason why, uniquely for a major South African city, only around one-quarter of Cape Town's population is 'African'. (I say 'partly' because, as Jared Diamond reminds us in his *Guns, Germs and Steel*, the Western Cape's winter rainfall meant that, while there were indigenous hunter-gatherers and pastoralists in occupation of this space over millennia, Bantu-speaking farming cultures were excluded by their dependence upon summer-rainfall crops.)

But there is also something else at play in the new elite's ambivalence about Cape Town.

I recently came across the following sentence in a website text dealing with South Africa's history and its 'peoples': 'The colonisers forced themselves on the native women, which brought in the Coloured race.' In other words, according to this view, over one-half of Cape Town's population ('the Coloured race') is the 'impure' progeny of 'colonial rape'.

This claim was not published in a tract by some recidivist white conservative organisation. It was on the website of a radical youth formation, overwhelmingly black in membership. It is a formation that would consider itself militantly progressive and eminently non-racial. The passage has since been removed from the website, and I will spare the organisation the embarrassment of direct referencing. The authors of this statement uncritically (unwittingly I am sure) repeat the ugliest of racial prejudices from the past. White racists routinely regarded 'Coloureds' as a 'bastard race', the result of 'depravity' and 'miscegenation'.

But what does this offending sentence, replayed now in the present, tell us? Is it a symptom of the legacy of uneven education, itself rooted in the persisting crises of underdevelopment in our society? Undoubtedly. But I suspect there is something more at stake. It is, perhaps, a fear that some implicit notion of race purity (and of the privileged victim status it underpins) might be challenged.

This fear is abetted by the tendency to elide the history of our country. Our memories of our past tend to be overwhelmed, understandably, by the drama of the more immediate apartheid era. But if you think of our present simply as post-apartheid, you might be inclined to forget Cape Town as an administrative outpost not so much of enforced racial apartness as of genocide. Through the golden years of colonial Cape Town, well into the nineteenth century, San/Bushman communities were systematically hunted down as vermin. In a matter of a few hundred years, civilisations that had occupied this space for millennia were exterminated. Of course, these peoples have not absolutely disappeared. Up behind Simon's Town Main Road, next to the waterfall, is a cave; like so many others it has yielded from its middens beautifully worked stone-scrapers and ostrich shell beads. The clicks of ancient civilisations continue to sound in the Nguni family of languages in our country, and, indeed, more and more in Cape Town as the long-collapsed peasant economies of the Eastern Cape create burgeoning squatter camps around the city. Most South Africans, black and white, still unknowingly evoke words borrowed from the disappeared peoples. Our most homely of interjections, '*eina!*' and '*sies!*', come to us from the Khoi, *e-na* and *tsi*. Genetically you can recognise the features of the disappeared all around us. They are even, surely, present in that most iconic of post-apartheid physiognomies – the genial face of Nelson Mandela.

From the beginnings of colonial settlement, from the mid-seventeenth century, Cape Town was also a slave capital. Slaves were shipped in from far and wide, Bengal and south India, Indonesia, Sri Lanka, Madagascar and the East and West African coasts. Some bequeathed to our city an unbroken, three-and-a-half-century Islamic tradition. The first book to be published in Cape Town was not in Dutch or English, but Arabic. To understand Cape Town, you would need also to add to this mix white working-class men and women, sailors, cooks, bartenders, blacksmiths and coopers rubbing shoulders at work with all and sundry, or white *bandieten* and ship-deserters ganging up with runaway slaves in *drosters*' caves. We should certainly not romanticise the pre-apartheid past of Cape Town, but neither should we lose sight of the proto-non-racialism that was forged unevenly in localities all about our city, as Capetonians went about their daily lives.

Abdullah Moses was born in Simon's Town in 1884. In the latter part of his life he could still recall a flourishing whaling industry that had operated out of Simon's Bay in his teenage years. As BB Brocks's *Historical Simon's Town* (1976) records his words:

On a Saturday morning a whale was sighted in Jaffer's Bay (Cole Point). The smoke signal was made and in next to no time the whaler Monarch, owned by Mr Hablutzel, put to sea with her crew consisting of Abdol Clark (harpooner), Jonkie Moses, Satarien Osborn, Agmat Jenkins, Sayed Solomons and Mr Marnewal (skipper). The whale was duly harpooned by Mr Abdol Clark. The line was allowed to run free and then secured to the bollard in the whaler. The whale towed the boat towards the open sea and took its first stop for a rest at a point about where the Dockyard Lighthouse now stands. It then pulled out along the coast in one long haul to Miller's Point.

I am pleased to say that the whale (the great-grandmother of the Southern Right whales that are now making their successful winter returns in ever-increasing numbers from Antarctica to breed, to birth, to breathe here in False Bay) eventually broke free. But listen to the names of the crew as they row out: 'Abdol Clark', 'Satarien Osborn', 'Agmat Jenkins', 'Marnewal' (but no Ajax among them).

Walk about Cape Town and you can still hear and see the undisappeared-disappeared, the multiphonic wrested from schizophrenia. Cape Town's subconscious has long guessed what contemporary science is now confirming: we are all the bearers of the same mixed-up genetic bredie. Humanity is Coloured. Our proto-non-racial Cape Town has always teetered on the brink of the possibilities of its Creole reality. And it is this reality that is, I think, such an important and corrective challenge to the dominant political discourse of our post-1994 South Africa.

It is a discourse of representative redistribution. 'Transformation' has come to mean *not* transformation but the elite redistribution of some racial, class and gendered power (whether in the boardroom or the Springbok rugby team). Representative individuals from formerly disadvantaged groups are the beneficiaries. Informing this politics are three

50

buttressing paradigms – an individualistic liberal rights politics (individuals are entitled to a slice of the action); an identity politics that posits relatively fixed and pre-given identities ('blackness' or 'African-ness', for instance); and a paradigm of democratic transformation that tends to reduce democracy to 'representation'. This is what, in poetics, we call 'metonymy', a part for the whole. In the new South Africa, a small number of 'representatives' enjoy new powers and privileges on behalf of the historically disadvantaged majority. This gives us an elite politics of racialised self-righteousness.

It is this dominant paradigm of our times that the mixed-ness, the Creole reality of Cape Town, disturbs. Cape Town's 'Coloured-ness', the fact that it is not 'really African' like South Africa's other major cities, constitutes a niggling problem for this discourse of representative redistribution which grounds so much of the politics of our time. For instance, how, as a newly enriched multimillionaire, do you continue to justify your ongoing benefit from 'black economic empowerment' deals? It is only by maintaining an equal sign (=) between yourself, the millionaire individual, and the historically (and still presently) disadvantaged majority that you can pull this off. And only the assumption of a fixed black identity will allow this. No wonder the history and present social reality of Cape Town have proven problematic.

The worthy idea of an African Renaissance, which has been a dominant theme of the Mbeki presidency, can also sometimes play into this new politics of elite self-righteousness. The European Renaissance could imagine itself rebirthing an earlier golden age of classical Greece and Rome, the age prefigured by Ajax ... the epic hero, brought to you by Homer (and not Hollywood, or Lever Brothers, or Colgate-Palmolive, or whatever the manufacturer of the foaming cleanser then was). But it is a short step between the idea of a re-naissance and the construction of some god-given and timeless European 'genius'. Likewise, the pursuit of an African Renaissance can have us scurrying backwards in search of some presumptive, authentic, pure, rooted and timeless African identity. The history and reality of Cape Town are likely to be disruptive of that pursuit.

But it will not be an effective disruption if we fall into a counteractive chauvinism, imagining a Cape Town rooted in the marriage of Europe and Asia to the exclusion of Africa. As I write, David Kramer and Taliep Petersen's wonderful show, *Ghoema*, is running at Cape Town's Baxter Theatre. It traces a cultural history of Cape Town through song and music. One of the most moving moments is Loukmaan Adams's rendition of *Sal Ik Dan*. It is a *Nederlandse liedjie* created at the Cape, fusing Dutch lyrics with an Eastern styling, bending notes and using a high-pitched nasal tone quality. It winds up and up and around, like a flock of homing pigeons exercising in the evening light as the southeaster drops for the night, and the imam calls the faithful to prayer from a mosque in Bo-Kaap. It is a song form known as a *karienkel*. The show *Ghoema* illustrates how slaves at the Cape created a musical idiom that fused the Portuguese *fado*, Dutch folk songs (*straatliederen*), Indonesian *krontjong*, sea shanties, and, later, Afro-American minstrel traditions. All of this is an enormously important part of a Cape Town cultural re-discovery. But, disappointingly, *Ghoema* barely alludes to the influence of indigenous Khoisan music and instruments, while other southern African musical traditions are totally absent. Has African music come to Cape Town only over the Atlantic and through the American minstrel tradition?

It is President Mbeki who has articulated one of the more moving celebrations of a new kind of South African identity, identity as process and not origin, identity as heterogeneity and not some univocal root, identity as mixed-ness:

I owe my being to the Khoi and the San whose desolate souls haunt the great expanses of the beautiful Cape – they who fell victim to the most merciless genocide our native land has ever seen … I am formed by the migrants who left Europe to find a new home on our native land. Whatever their own actions, they remain still part of me. In my veins courses the blood of the Malay slaves who came from the East. Their proud dignity informs my bearing, their culture is part of my essence … I am the grandchild of the warrior men and women that Hintsa and Sekhukhune led, the patriots that Cetshwayo and Mhephu took to battle, the soldiers Moshoeshoe and Ngungunyane taught never to dishonour the cause of freedom … I am the grandchild who lays fresh flowers on the Boer graves at St Helena and the Bahamas … I come of those who were transported from India and China, whose being resided in the fact, solely, that they were able to provide physical labour, who taught me that we could both be at home and be foreign …

Mbeki delivered this justly celebrated speech on the occasion of the adoption of South Africa's new constitution in May 1996. He titled it: 'I am an African'.

'I am an African' … the chorus in my head starts to murmur. I take out my Criterion bioscope lucky-draw winning ticket. I've kept it from the late 1950s. It's a ticket that entitles me to stay on in this imaginary Cape Town. 'I am an African' … I think about that with the voice of the balcony chorus buzzing in my head. 'I … am … an African' … and the chorus wants to respond (not with a dismissive 'Da foaming cleanser'), but with a query.

What if Mbeki had said: 'I am a Coloured'? How subversive, how transformational, how right that might have been. Then again, how open to misinterpretation it could be ...

But that's the chorus in my head. You can choose to ignore it, if you will.

Jeremy Cronin spent most of his childhood in and around Cape Town. He attended the University of Cape Town and later lectured there. He was active in the underground anti-apartheid movement, and spent seven years as a political prisoner in Pretoria Maximum Security Prison. He currently lives in Cape Town with his family, and is an ANC Member of Parliament and Deputy General Secretary of the South African Communist Party. His publications include four collections of poetry.

Henrietta Rose-Innes

Five Sites

Beyond the beach at Sandy Bay, the coastline becomes rocky, leading out to a narrow peninsula. Boulders lie jumbled on top of rock shelves, which tilt down to submerged mussel-beds. It seems an inhospitable place, windswept and hard to negotiate; several ships have left wreckage off the coast here. But it is peaceful, and there is shelter if you know where to find it.

The granite boulders erode into hollow spheres, some big enough to sit or stand in. One such cave, out on the peninsula, is probably used by perlemoen or crayfish poachers. It is neat, quite clean and well kitted-out, with a handy rock shelf and doorposts of driftwood. Closer to the beach, there is a large boulder that has split right open, revealing a hollow centre. Inside, the rock is smeared with blackened molten plastic. On the sandy floor are mussel shells and a threadbare blue jersey, flattened and stiff with salt. Outside, rusted tin cans have been tidily deposited in a crack in the rock. It seems the rock broke open recently, probably due to the intense heat of the plastic fire. It must have been a shock to whomever was keeping warm inside.

*Then there's Stan's cave, on the path from the beach and thus the easiest to find. It's the most elaborate of the three, extended with crude walls of stone and sandy mortar, now half collapsed. Outside are some rusty half-drums that may once have held water. Scattered inside are, among other things, piles of old magazines (*Your Pregnancy*), two tin cups, stompies, crayfish antennae, three mismatched running shoes in small sizes, and more mussel shells. 'EAGLE'S CAVE' is written in pink paint above the cave entrance. Propped to one side is a driftwood plank, on which is a weathered inscription in black ink. It begins:*

Hi There
Welcome to Eagle's Cave
Which is also my home
I live off the sea and proceeds of the sales of my artworks.
Some folk have been kind ... willing (?illegible)...
... as well as donations of clothing and food ...

There are no 'artworks' in evidence. 'STAN 1989' is painted on a boulder outside the cave, half of the 'S' overgrown with lichen. The place is a mess, but the cigarette butts and plastic bottles have probably been left here by others since Stan made his exit. Perhaps in his time Stan was tidy; house-proud.

People make homes in unlikely places – where there should be no homes, where nobody is supposed to live. Eccentric, isolated constructions on the urban fringes, with no official permission asked or granted. I'll call them 'sites' because they remind me of archaeological sites: places that vanished inhabitants once marked out as theirs, that mutely present the physical evidence of lives.

As at archaeological sites, I feel little of the usual distaste for human litter. In the context of a special 'site'

– circumscribed by the walls of a cave, an enclosure of branches, a circle of stones – the cigarette packets and empty bottles become intriguing artefacts, clues. Neither do I feel a sense of intrusion into these private, melancholy spaces. Like the long-dead occupants of ancient caves, the disembodied inhabitants of these more recent sites would surely not resent me. They have left their homes open, without lock or key, as if for me to find.

Nonetheless, the sites are secret. Of course, I know that others are aware of them – but only a few, I like to believe. I feel a responsibility to keep their locations somewhat obscure; to not show them to too many people, or signpost them too precisely.

These places are generally inconvenient to get to, but not so far from the city as to cut off a meagre flow of commodities: they usually contain the remnants of cigarettes, matches, candles, liquor, newspapers, cardboard for sleeping. Some have clearly never been full-time dwellings, but are more like camps or shrines. One sees in their design the hand of eccentric, creative, perhaps disturbed souls. These solitary architects have accepted hardship and exposure to live this way. Perhaps they are unable to thrive in the city, or have been chased away. Perhaps they have visions, tortured or brilliant, that can only be realised in isolation.

The little inlet is almost invisible from the road, and it's a hard scramble down the slope to get there. To arrive by boat is possible but also difficult, as the shore is rocky and the waves rough. The bay is a magnet for flotsam of all kinds: we've found dead seals, a dead dog, wave-worn flip-flops and plastic bottles. And driftwood: planks, stripped branches, burnt hunks that have been smoothed by the waves to look like meteorites. Above the stones and churning waves of the bay there is a small grove of milkwoods, a patch of soft grass. A stream flows down to the sea through the reeds and grasses; it's always flowing, even on the hottest days. Tour boats sometimes pass within sight of shore, but they never approach.

Under the milkwoods, someone has created a camp, with reclining chairs of elaborate design, a table and shelves, all made out of silvery driftwood. For a time, there were two hammocks made of green fishing net hanging here. These furnishings are in flux. Every time we go there, something has changed: new items have been added, old ones have vanished, something different has washed up on the shore. Once, we arrived with bread and cheese but no knife; within minutes we'd found a worn blade, attached to a fisherman's float, lodged among the wrack. Sometimes we take something with us when we leave: an attractive stone, a piece of driftwood. Nothing too big, because it's a very steep walk back up a crumbling slope.

There is no sense of trespass. We don't know who else uses this place; perhaps fishermen, perhaps idlers like ourselves. Whoever they are, they don't visit often: between visits, grass grows through the hearth and over the legs of the ingenious wooden chairs. Everyone who uses this camp seems to leave it clean.

The solitude of this site is threatened by plans to build a 'boutique hotel' a little way along the coastline. Not very close, but near enough that restless 'boutique' tourists might stumble upon this camp and spoil it. If this happens we'll probably stop coming here.

Handmade homes built with found materials are nothing unusual – the informal settlements consist of them. In niches within the formal city, too, these dwellings exist, like the small community that used to live under the snapped-off flyover on the Foreshore. The smoke from cooking fires came drifting up between the cars on the off-ramp during rush hour. And every time I drive along the highway to the southern suburbs, I glance at the neat homestead that somebody's erected below the bridge at Observatory. Right next to the roaring traffic, there's a fire going, a house, piles of firewood, dogs, even plastic garden furniture. Flying past, I can't see the inhabitants clearly or pick up more than a general impression; but I can see that the place has the confidence of an established settlement. And then, much more tenuous, there are the pavement beds of the homeless. I look away when I pass these places, because it is rude to stare in through people's bedroom windows, however notional. I do not stop to explore, sitting in chairs or lying in beds. These homes – poor, but actively inhabited – are not my sites.

My places are different. They are unpeopled, at least when I'm there. Their emptiness is their appeal. No doubt, if Stan were still in his cave, I would have avoided it in the first place; would have resisted a personal encounter. I don't like to meet other people in wild places. But Stan is gone; and, although not exactly picturesque with its accumulation of cans and bottles, his cave has been sanitised by time and sea air. None of my sites has the musky smell of ongoing habitation. This makes them less intimidating, more approachable. These dwellings are like dried-out shells from which the meat of the shellfish has long vanished; I can crawl inside and take the place of the original occupant. Some of these sites I've slept in, eaten in, lived in for a few hours or a night – and in doing so, have achieved a kind of intimacy with the absent one. I swing in the hammock that someone else suspended. I make a fire in the abandoned hearth. I place my hands where other hands have been, sit against rocks worn smooth by other backs. For this moment, I am the resident. The next person to come past may in turn find ashes or an apple-core, and briefly imagine me.

Again, this kind of close connection is something I have felt, or imagined, in very old human habitations, ancient rock shelters. Such places have a deep familiarity: a place for fire, a place to sleep, water nearby. The human essentials. Feeding a small fire with a stick of wood, I could be living five hundred years ago; five thousand.

Not far from the commonly used paths in Newlands Forest, there is a grove of particularly dense indigenous forest. The place is always quite hard to find, because I get confused about which of the similar switchback gravel paths approaches the spot, and because the vegetation grows back quickly and obscures the faint track that leads to the tree house. Once we tried to mark the track with a red stone, but the next time the stone was overgrown, or had been removed. When we first visited here, the structure emerged unexpectedly, magically from the trees. We came across the twisted monkey-ropes and realised suddenly that they weren't natural: they'd been skilfully knotted. Straight branches had been lashed together to form a kind of palisade. Someone had woven a house around the twisting limbs of a huge old tree.

It was peaceful inside the leafy shelter. We found candle stubs, and some strong, worn tools – clippers, pliers – hidden under a plank seat. In the next-door tree, we discovered a cunningly constructed staircase made of knotted lianas that allowed one to climb up the almost vertical trunk into the canopy, where platforms had been constructed. It was too high and precarious for me to try, but I'm told that up there were several well-watered dagga plants in pots. Further into the undergrowth, we found a couple more plants concealed.

We never found out who'd built this hideout: it seemed so audacious, within shouting distance of the well-worn dog-walkers' paths. Once, appearing suddenly out of the trees, we startled some stoned teenagers there; but they seemed too uneasy for the place to belong to them. Some years before, alone in the forest, I'd walked into a kind of artwork: slats of wood arranged around a tree trunk in an elegant, organic spiral. This shelter felt like it might have come from the same skilled hands.

A year or so after we first discovered the tree house, it was destroyed, presumably by park wardens. When we saw it next, the carefully lashed branches had been torn down and the dagga plants were all gone, although the monkey-rope stairway still led up the tree trunk to nowhere.

We have found these shelters through no deliberate effort. Often, I've simply stumbled on them by following my own impulses. The locations that their hidden makers have selected are the same places that I would choose: my own dreams of solitude and retreat draw me to that same rock, that grove of trees, that outlook. I too have a fantasy of finding a secret hideout – one that is here in Cape Town, but which exists simultaneously in another place, somewhere less controlled and familiar. These sites all have a strong sense of overlapping universes: wild and tame, new and ancient, real and fairy-tale.

Between the last line of houses in Oranjezicht and Tafelberg Road, there is a stretch of steep, rough land, bordering on Deer Park. The vegetation makes me uneasy. There is a lot of alien growth, which together with the litter makes the area feel both tainted and neglected, not quite part of the mountain; thus threatening. Here, under the low trees, I find a hollow in the grass, some charred newspapers, an empty brandy bottle. I am nervous because I am alone; and because there is less personality and more need expressed in these frugal traces than at the other sites. Whoever made this den had nothing, almost no possessions at all. No jaunty written signs or whimsical weaving of wood and lianas. However, this little encampment too expresses the basics of human existence: fire, shelter, sustenance.

Other cities have their own eccentric dwellings, their live-in outsider art. But Cape Town, built between accessible semi-wildernesses of mountain and seaside, has softer, more porous edges than most urban areas – edges that allow the odd solitary soul to be absorbed, to disappear. Such sites can be confusing, disorientating. They extend the city into the fringes of the wild, but they also bring the wildness closer to home, blurring the transition.

To enter these sites is to confront several, perhaps particularly South African, impulses and constraints: distrust and fear of strangers, but also a deep curiosity about the way they live; an unwillingness or inability to experience others in their intimate settings; the strangeness and excitement of doing so. Lacking the usual clues, it is hard to make the standard assumptions, to identify the race or class of the site-makers. They remain mysterious, invisible, people who have erased themselves or been erased from the scene. As outsiders or eccentrics, they may already have rejected communities, identities. One can guess only that they are mostly male, as solitary women in these places would be very vulnerable.

Many of these sites superficially resemble slum dwellings, in their construction and in the material poverty of the lifestyles they reveal; they trigger signals of warning and avoidance in the mind of the middle-class visitor. But they are also situated in some of the loveliest places in the city, and there is a corresponding tug of attraction, of homecoming. To sit at someone else's hearth, watching the waves break against the rocks only metres away, is to experience simultaneously the thrill of trespass and the pleasure of coming to nature. At these sites that are both urban and wild, it is the wildness, paradoxically, that reassures. Wilderness is safer than a hostile zone of the city.

But the beaches and mountain slopes of Cape Town are not really wildernesses, and are becoming less so. Muggings and attacks happen frequently now in these peri-urban areas, and I don't feel safe exploring these places alone. Five years ago, I was more confident. Perhaps, these days, fewer hermits dare attempt life in the margins. Physical threat may be one of the reasons that vulnerable people like Stan have abandoned their modest homes in caves and forests. Dreams of retreat into idyllic wilderness crumble when the wilderness turns out to be not as uninhabited as imagined, nor as gentle.

The small hut is next to the dirt track that runs along the fence of the Cape Point Nature Reserve, in sight of Scarborough's houses but removed from them. The old man who lived here and in the rusty caravan outside was a hermit of sorts. He was killed, I've been told, by local boys, perhaps because there was a rumour that he kept his life savings under his bed. The place has been completely trashed, the contents disgorged, rained and urinated on. Outside, someone has made a small memorial, a modest heap of stones. Inside the caravan are piles and piles of books and magazines – Reader's Digest, Woman's Value *– all years old. I pick up a few small coloured tiles, the kind used in bathrooms, and a small pocket-size volume of Machiavelli's* The Prince, *which I take away with me. The site is unbearably sad. It must once have been a beautiful place to live.*

Like grand old houses that have been abandoned and are falling into disrepair, these dwellings can be places of poignancy and loss: these, too, were dream homes once.

Or perhaps they simply represent failure, exclusion, want. Those who have claimed a place in the world do not allow trespassers to open their doors and peek inside. And they stay, they are not routed; their homes are not left open to the weather.

But my sites can also provoke a childlike surprise and delight. They can seem like play houses, fairy-tale homes. They are an expression of the oldest human prerogative: the desire to make one's own place, with basic materials, with fundamental human skills. And they represent a kind of defiance – of the municipality and the parks board; of conventional community; of the forces that decide who may live in the choicest parts of Cape Town and who may not; of the uniformity of built houses, the ostentation of housing estates, the authority of architects, the conceit of brick and mortar.

A new development is creeping up the dunes high above Sandy Bay, on the opposite side of the nek to Stan's folly. There are dozens of huge houses here, brand new, un-occupied or occupied only in the summer holidays. Through burglar-alarmed windows it is possible to peer in at empty rooms. They are fitted with stoves and fridges and expensive finishes. But they have no ghosts, no unique artefacts, no secret story. They do not let me in.

> ... *Feel free to rest up & look around & enjoy the best view*
>   *in Cape Town.*
> *Thank you for stopping by and having a chat.*
> *Enjoy the rest of your day*
> *God Bless*
> *Stan*

Henrietta Rose-Innes was born in 1971 in Cape Town, where she still lives. Her first novel, *Shark's Egg*, was published in 2000, and *The Rock Alphabet* appeared in 2004. She has a BSc (Hons) and an MA in Creative Writing from the University of Cape Town, and currently works as a literary editor.

Mike Nicol

The City I Live In

1: An Approach

In the old diagrams and panoramas of Cape Town, the road into the settlement appears over the lower slopes of Devil's Peak, widening as it approaches the Castle. Where Strand Street will be are beach and sand dunes and closer to the Castle is a landing jetty. A panorama produced by the German soldier Johannes Schumacher in 1778 shows a sandy road crossing a small stream before it enters at a wooden stockade under the southern bastion of Katzenellenbogen. Within the defensive battery that parallels the shoreline, the road continues under the Castle wall, round the Buuren bastion past the gate to the Leerdam bastion where it divides

---

For the historical detail included in this essay, I am indebted to Nigel Penn's *Rogues, Rebels and Runaways* (1999), and to Nigel Worden, Elizabeth van Heyningen and Vivian Bickford-Smith's *Cape Town: The Making of a City* (1998).

into paths leading towards the town. Schumacher also shows a wide sandy road heading up the mountain. Not far from the Castle battlement and off this road, he has drawn a rectangle: a low wall enclosing a piece of land with no other apparent features.

Entering the city now along this road is a bleak walk down New Market Street with the slatted concrete fence of the railway yards on the right until the pavement opens unexpectedly onto bright lawns dotted with palm trees. Apart from bergies, there are no pedestrians. No local would think to walk here for pleasure despite the trees and the inviting grass where children could chase and romp. It is as it once was: an approach to the city that is now a transit zone of bridges, underpasses and railway lines.

On Schumacher's panorama the road is white and empty: two small houses stand on the seaward side shortly after a track that leads up the mountain to a farm where today University Estate gazes across the bay. On this mild winter day before a storm, a man lies asleep on the grass of New Market Street, warmed by the sun. From where he is stretched out he would not be able to see the walls of the Castle through the stanchions of the flyovers, yet the city's oldest building is no more than three or four hundred metres away. At this junction, under the Oswald Pirow bridge and the Eastern Boulevard flyover, where New Market ends and Strand Street begins, is, on the left, an empty zone, damp and cold, at the back of the Good Hope Centre; on the right, the bland entrance to Cape Town station for trains on the peninsula line. Under the flyover are signs of habitation: flattened cardboard boxes, tins, bottles, the remains of a fire. All traces of the small stream and the entrance stockade are long gone beneath a cluster of buildings erected during the Castle's military days and surrounded by tall wire fences. Beyond are the Katzenellenbogen bastion and Strand Street's four lanes of traffic, bordered on one side by the blank wall of the station and on the other by the wide swathe of littered grass below the Castle wall. During weekdays parked cars line the Castle side of the street and in today's sunny winter weather groups of bergies have gathered on the grass to drink and sleep. Rounding Buuren into Buitenkant Street, passing coaches of tourists headed for the Castle gate, the road leads beneath Leerdam and across Darling Street. On the left the ground rises and beneath this nondescript part of the city with its vacant plots, car park and sad buildings lies the walled rectangle on Schumacher's panorama: the place of execution, the *justitie plaats*. At any time in the first hundred and fifty years, people heading for the settlement would have passed the remains of the punished, perhaps they would have quickened their pace along the final stretch to the town. A drawing in the William Fehr Collection housed in the Castle shows two gallows with figures hanging from the gibbets and a wheel where those sentenced to be 'broken' were tied down and their bones smashed. The drawing, dated at the beginning of the eighteenth century, places the gallows beneath the ominous heights of Devil's Peak. The siting was deliberate: the broken bodies of the punished were a warning to all travellers of how transgressions would be dealt with.

2: The Hidden Pattern

Johannes Schumacher stood on Signal Hill to draw his panoramic view of the town: a grand vista that showed the high ravined face of the flat-topped mountain, the encircling buttress of Devil's Peak, a tranquil bay where seven large trading ships and several smaller schooners and barques waited in the roadstead. Between the mountain and the sea lay the neat double-storey houses of the burghers and the merchants. Schumacher's panorama further depicts a town laid out on a formal grid of streets, the homes of the burghers clustered neatly into square blocks of between ten and twelve houses. The streets that will become Shortmarket, Longmarket, Church, and Wale traverse the town north to south; at ninety degrees to them are the streets that will be named Plein, Adderley, St George's, Burg, Long, Loop, and Bree. At the outer limits are Buitenkant (running down to the Castle) and Buitengracht (below Signal Hill): the town neatly enclosed, imposed upon an alien landscape. Above the town are the ordered rows of the Company Gardens, also carefully segmented into blocks, and beyond small farms climbing the lower slopes of what will later be known as the City Bowl. Below Signal Hill Schumacher's panorama also shows two graveyards surrounded by low white walls outside the Buitengracht and some distance from the shore. In the cemetery closest to the Buitengracht are buried free burghers, in the other, slaves.

From Signal Hill today the pattern of the settlement and early town is hidden by the tower blocks of the central business district and yet it is still there to the discerning eye: the grid designed by the officials of the Dutch East India Company continues to shape the modern city. So to walk in the streets of Cape Town is to walk in the colonial town and the Company's settlement. To cross the Grand Parade is to stroll over the open ground that once separated the Castle from the town or to move between the marching platoons celebrating the birthday of Queen Victoria or to edge through the crowds waiting for the release of Nelson Mandela. To walk from the Castle gateway keeping outside the moat and under the bastion of Leerdam over the intersection of Buitenkant with Darling, then left up the rise of Longmarket to its corner with Harrington Street, is to follow a route taken by people sentenced to death. People who suffered gruesome executions with the magnificent mountain in their eyes. One such was the young slave woman Trijntje of Madagascar – found guilty of 'matters of evil and dangerous consequence' which included trying to poison her mistress and killing her own child.

In 2004, looking down from Signal Hill, almost three hundred years after Trijntje's execution, could be seen, on the corner of Prestwich and Chiappini streets, a building site enclosed by a makeshift fence constructed from sheets of corrugated iron. The building that had been demolished to make way for a block of apartments with lofts which would have views into the Waterfront and back towards Table Mountain, had been a warehouse and, in more recent years, a club where garage and house music thundered through the small hours of most weekends. The ravers did not know they were dancing on the bones of the dead. Once the old structure was demolished, excavation for the underground parking and foundations of the loft apartments began, revealing, just beneath the surface, the skeletons of old Cape Town. These skeletons were thought to be the remains of slaves, and might well include the bones of Trijntje's child. If that was the second cemetery, then, following Schumacher's panorama, a block to the south, say, under the buildings on the corner of Somerset Road and Chiappini and Prestwich streets, must lie the first graveyard and in it, I imagine, the bones of Trijntje's mistress, Elizabeth Lingelbach, who ran a coffee shop during the opening years of the eighteenth century, and eventually died a peaceful death.

3: The Soil of Cape Town

Elizabeth Lingelbach lived in one of the two hundred

and fifty-four whitewashed houses that made up the blocks and grid of the Company's settlement. In 1714, the traveller François Valentyn thought the houses attractive and ornamental, while a few years previously Johanna van Riebeeck, the granddaughter of the founding commander Jan van Riebeeck, had considered it a 'miserable place'. 'There is no grass,' she noted, 'and the roads near the Castle and in the town are covered with holes and ruts, as if wild pigs had been rooting in them ... There is nothing pretty to be seen along the shoreline ... the Castle is very peculiar ... the other houses here resemble prisons ... One sees here all sorts of peculiar people who live in very strange ways.'

Into the whitewashed prison-like ornamental house of Elizabeth Lingelbach was brought the slave Trijntje of Madagascar, a young woman in her early twenties. Trijntje had been at the Cape since 1696. As a child of about eight years old, she'd been bought at the mouth of Madagascar's Maningaer River during a slaving expedition by a Dutch slave trader, and resold at the settlement. Twelve years later she was bought by Elizabeth Lingelbach and joined a household of peculiar people who lived in a very strange way.

Elizabeth Lingelbach was married but she didn't stay with her husband, the brewer Willem Menssink. Mostly she didn't stay with Menssink because he abused her and lusted after young slave women and on one occasion Elizabeth awoke in the night to find her husband sandwiched between herself and his favourite slave. On other occasions she found them consorting in the attic, on another in the dairy, and when she came across him cavorting with two slave women in the stables, Elizabeth Lingelbach moved back to her mother's house. But Menssink would not let her be: he took up with a slave woman in the Lingelbach household and was caught with her by Elizabeth, first in the attic and then in a laundry cupboard. The woman was sold, another one bought. Menssink had his way with her too.

On the death of her mother, Elizabeth inherited the coffee shop and bought Trijntje of Madagascar. Two nights later, Trijntje was approached by the suggestive Menssink. She turned him down. The next night Menssink tried again, and Trijntje, well aware of Menssink's relationship with her mistress and his important status in the settlement as the brewer, let him have his way. But that night stirred an obsession in Menssink, enslaving them both in a love affair mad and destructive, which, in his account of the very strange ways of this household, the historian Nigel Penn called 'the fatal passion of brewer Menssink'.

This fatal passion lasted for four years and included Menssink and Trijntje having sex in every room of Elizabeth's house from the cellar to the attic. He would reach it by a tall ladder carried through the dark streets on the backs of his two faithful slaves, Gerrit and Isaac, and placed so that he had access through the attic window. It was then taken away and returned in the small hours when Menssink would climb down and hurry home. He also had sex with Trijntje in Elizabeth's room at the foot of his estranged wife's bed while she lay asleep (having been dusted by the pair with a yellow and white powder that Elizabeth later came to believe was ground-up human bones). Arrangements of this sort lasted for a year, Trijntje falling pregnant during that time and Menssink deciding to have her administer a potion of powder and hair to Elizabeth in an attempt to poison his wife. It came to nothing although after the birth of Trijntje and Menssink's son – called 'the mongrel' by Elizabeth – they renewed their attempts to poison her with a mixture of hair and kapok (a wild cotton) that also came to include the powdered bones of the dead, nail clippings and the scrapings of roots. To strengthen the powers of this potion they snatched a human hand from the scaffolds at the place of execution where the bodies of the punished rotted away. They buried it in the ground close to Elizabeth's bedroom with Menssink simultaneously strengthening the poison until Elizabeth took ill and Trijntje took pity and fright, fleeing to a shelter at Lion's Head from which she would steal down the mountain each night to Menssink's bedroom. It was a situation that lasted for ten months before she returned to Elizabeth's household to kill her son and poison her mistress – the latter becoming sicker and sicker until, in the early summer of 1712, the authorities intervened to arrest the distraught and crazed Trijntje of Madagascar.

She, Gerrit and Isaac were incarcerated in the Castle's Leerdam bastion and Menssink was placed under house arrest. By the time the three slaves stood trial in March the following year, Menssink had wriggled away and was brewing beer at Newlands without a thought for the woman who had fired in him a dangerous passion and without a moment's regard for the loyal men who had enabled his nightly escapades. In a judgment read from the Kat balcony inside the Castle, Gerrit was sentenced to stand with the gallow's rope round his neck and then to be whipped and branded on his back. He was further condemned to be shackled and sent to labour on Robben Island for twenty-five years. As he was already in his forties he must have died on the island. Isaac faced the whip and the branding iron, after which he was to be placed in chains and sent to the island for three years. Trijntje was sentenced to death.

Two days after sentence was delivered, the three were brought up from the dungeons and placed in an open cart for the short ride to the place of execution, with members of the Court of Justice, a company of soldiers, and a crowd of burghers, sailors, and slaves following. Menssink was not among the bystanders; nor was Elizabeth.

Trijntje, Gerrit and Isaac had all been born thousands

of kilometres away from this inauspicious settlement, at the time known simply as 'the Cape', as had Elizabeth and Menssink. Yet it had gathered them up and brought them to this sorry pass, which for Trijntje now meant a violent death. As the cart trundled below Leerdam did a southeaster whip up sand, forcing her to squint against the wind and late summer glare, until, at the entrance to the *plaats*, the party stopped, the burghers drawing back in a half circle? Did she think of herself when, as a girl, she'd been torn from her family to be sold on the river bank? Did she wonder at the demented passion that had so ruled her heart? While a short prayer was said, did she search for Menssink's face in the crowd?

Of the *justitie plaats* a traveller recorded:

Drawing near the place of execution we beheld a horrid spectacle. Upon the sands were erected a number of stakes and gibbets upon which were the remains of upward of a dozen malefactors who had been executed at the Cape at different periods. Some were suspended by the feet, decapitated: others were laid across the narrow wheel on which they had been racked, bent double and hanging down on each side, whilst many seemed to preserve by the attitude in which they were placed, the last writhing of pain and approaching death.

Trijntje stood at the place of execution and listened to the howls of pain as first Gerrit then Isaac had the skin flayed from their backs. With the stench of their branded flesh prickling in her nostrils, the trembling woman faced her executioners. She was bound to a pole. She could smell the ocean; she could feel the wind; she could see the roiling clouds. A cord was looped round her neck and drawn tight. She gagged, fighting the rising panic before the desperate heaves for breath tore at her chest and the mountain swam in her eyes. Her body convulsed against the ropes and knots holding her; her face turned livid in a rushing darkness. Then she was still; the executioner released the strangle cord and her head flopped forward.

The young woman's body was cut down and fastened to a forked post and left for the seagulls to pick out her eyes and the jackals and rats to scavenge her flesh. Eventually Trijntje of Madagascar was subsumed into the soil of Cape Town.

4: A Smell from the Sea

At the start of winter I stood on Signal Hill at a spot where Schumacher might have stood as he carefully composed his panorama. About me, tourists with digital cameras tried to capture the same panorama, dividing the sweep of the mountain, the town, the sea, into segments. From here the Castle was obscured by tall buildings, although we could see the high ground beside it where Schumacher had drawn the faint rectangle of the place of execution. The Eastern Boulevard, the road into the city, was strung with cars, and in the roadstead were as many ships as Schumacher had depicted. In the distance a plane lowered from the northern sky probably with eager visitors peering out at the Cape's dangerous beauty. I wondered what it would be like to see the city with foreign eyes or to hear it as a story told by a tour guide: a story apart? That morning Cape Town smelt of fish and the sea, a tang that always brings back my childhood and memories of my grandparents in their Victoria Court flat at the top of Long Street. There is this about the city I live in: the buildings hold us; the streets shape our lives. Here, smell is memory and the bones are beneath our feet. The soil is human.

Mike Nicol works as a journalist. He has also written novels, among them *The Powers That Be*, some books of non-fiction, and poetry. He lives in Cape Town.

Jenefer Shute

The Annotated Guide

I turn my back for twenty-five years, and what happens? Cape Town becomes a destination. Pasty Londoners hold their weddings there, dour Swedes inspect Robben Island, space-starved New Yorkers panic in the cable cars. Cuisine occurs. Guidebooks are written.

The unofficial totem of this new Cape Town, I discover, is *the African penguin, a species formerly known as the jackass penguin.* They look cute on a T-shirt, now that they're African. Humans swamp their habitat to see them. And half a million pilgrims flock each year to a former prison island, once also a leper colony.

I return, guidebook in hand – having become, in the meanwhile, one of those New Yorkers, dizzied by light. I need a map to find my way around. Can this really be the city where I lived for four years, a Cape Town as grey and grainy as newsprint in my mind? Perhaps I am merely remembering the newsprint itself. Perhaps you remember it too, the newsprint of the mid-Seventies, grim and urgent and mute. Inklings so bad you knew the truth must be terrible.

The covers of my guidebooks are resplendently blue – mountain, sea, sky – but I don't recognise the sparkling place they promise me. My Cape Town was dismal, inclement; it drizzled, it raged, it poured. Atrocity was our weather, it walled us in. *Huis clos*, the city seemed to say: no way out. And, despite the Cape Doctor, not enough air.

Getting There and Away
Many international flights in and out of the city are available

For the settler, of course, life is always elsewhere. So, in 1978, I unsettled myself. I lived in various cities, some blue, some grey, alighting at last in Manhattan. Life, in spite of everything, happened to me.

What had driven me from Cape Town had been the conviction that I was living in a dying world, a benighted society clinging, in terminal condition and in defiance of history, to the tip of Africa. As it turned out, I was wrong – gratefully so. But in New York, after September 11, a similar conviction overtook me. Another benighted society, defiant and besieged, clinging this time to a tiny island.

My native land, by contrast, suddenly seemed open and free. The irony was not lost on me that, in 2003, more civil liberties were guaranteed on the tip of Africa than in the US of A. That the soldiers with the dogs and machine guns were in the subways of New York, not the streets of Guguletu. So I travelled back, nineteen hours in steerage. And I brought my guides with me, the *Rough* and the *Lonely* and all the rest: I knew I would be lost.

Now there are too many Cape Towns, at least three coexisting in my head, competing for space: the grainy Cape Town of the 1970s, the virtual Cape Town of the guidebooks, and the place where, arriving at last, jet-lagged and hyperstimulated, unmoored in time, I walk, drive, breathe the air. Yes, there's air now, wind, ozone, the tang of something I think might be fynbos. And hordes of alien invaders, disembarking this time from widebody jets.

Bring plenty of film
In this beautiful city even transient visitors can't help but devote
a few million brain cells to storing images of its grandeur

Perhaps, back then, I didn't have a few million neurons to spare. Perhaps I performed a cerebral wipe/delete at thirty-five thousand feet, en route from what was then DF Malan Airport, to clear space for a new continent. But, more likely, I chose to store as little as possible in the first place. Travel light, I told myself, take only what you need, hoard nothing that could break your heart.

How can you know at eighteen or twenty-two – or, for that matter, at fifty – what will break your heart?

Searching in old shoeboxes, I discover that, besides some letters and ancient news clippings, all that remains is three photos: A former lover, now in Australia, next to a tree at Rhodes Mem. My graduation from UCT, where I'm looking windblown and confused. Myself and someone's Ducati 750 on Chapman's Peak Drive, *a thrilling journey and one of the most beautiful drives in the world.* Why these particular images, I couldn't say – the accidents of the mail and too many moves. They have, as photos will, usurped memory, the less reliable lunar caustic. Besides, the apparatus was malfunctioning, light wasn't getting in. Like so many of us, I survived – if you could call it that – by cultivating an inner, proleptic absence.

Now, like a hallucination, the city is crystalline, magically blue. It hurts my eyes to look at it.

As big cities go, Cape Town is small

The guidebooks offer a menu of locales: the City Centre, the Waterfront, the Southern Suburbs, Table Mountain, the Atlantic Seaboard, the False Bay Seaboard, the Whale Coast, the Winelands. There's also Gay Cape Town and Backpackers' Cape Town and Kids' Cape Town. Cosmetic Surgery Cape Town. Where, I wonder, are all these places (and – wipe/delete – which seaboard is which)? Could they be inventions or perhaps even installations of the tourist board? Only one, as it turns out – the Waterfront, wholly factitious and irreal, a mirage of global consumerism, fabricated, or so it seems, from a blank space on the map.

My Cape Town was pathetically small, a narrow circuit from UCT to Rondebosch, to Rosebank, Mowbray, Obs, with occasional expeditions to the Labia or the Space. A radius, all told, of six kilometres. I had no car in those days, got around (I think) by bus. I must have used the trains too but remember only the buses, their interiors always misted, in my mind, from the damp. Now, in dazzling sunlight, I zip around the city in a rented Toyota – but on the wrong side, the mirror side, of the street, convinced at every turn that I am about to crash and die. That I will disappear into the past, dwindling, like a switched-off TV, to a pinpoint of light.

Any destination that takes more than four songs on the radio to reach is widely considered, in Cape Town parlance, to be 'a bit of a mission'

How many songs, I wonder, to New York? To Boston, Los Angeles, and all the other places I have lived?

You can't really call yourself a traveller until you've been to the top of Table Mountain

The mountain reinscribes itself against the sky, topography turned logo. When I lived in Cape Town I took it for granted: a movie-set by day, a hologram by night, backdrop to my inner drama and to our quotidian theatre of the absurd. Once, with relatives from Joburg, I rode up in a cable car, gazed out at a bowl of dense fog, grew bored and chilled. I had no interest in Nature then – only books and ideas, prison breaks – but now, after too many years in Manhattan, I do. Manhattan has made me hungry for light and air, for unparcelled space. For the first time, I feel compelled not only to reach the top of the mountain but – for want of a better word – to master it, to make it mine.

I climb it, the easy way, avoiding Skeleton Gorge. It takes a good few hours; on the level path atop the massif, I have the sense of having arrived somewhere. The Cape extends itself glittering around me. Now, perhaps, I can call myself a traveller. Now, perhaps, I can breathe.

Glossary
just now   *in a while*

There's always an accident on Hospital Bend. But that's not what I'm thinking about as I round it now, past the blind, bland (and, yes, shabby) sweep of Groote Schuur. I'm thinking about the interior of the hospital. And not about the heart transplant, either. I'm thinking about the seventeen-year-old girl who ended up there in 1974, after a close encounter with a baton-wielding member of the SAP. As I lay there for ten days, heavily sedated and unable to move, I listened to the cars speeding by on De Waal Drive and swore that, once out in the world again, among the living, I'd never pass the hospital without thinking of the people inside. Now, twenty-five years later, I think of them. And one of them, I can't help feeling, is that seventeen-year-old still.

There are also recreations of the scrub room and of the patient, Mr Louis Washkansky, lying in ICU. Unfortunately, he died eighteen days after the procedure, but his heart is still on display in the museum

I find my way back – magnetically, like a migrant bird – to my former, and, I assume, vanished habitat. But, to my horror, Rondebosch looks exactly the same – only, if anything, seedier and more depressed. Except for the rampant fast-food chains, I recognise, or think I recognise, the same drab landmarks of twenty-five years ago, even – can this be possible? – the same Coca-Cola sign at the station café. There they all still are, as if preserved in some private museum: the Pick 'n Pay, the chemist, the café, the book shop, the shoe shop, the flower-seller, the traffic lights persisting in their same illogical cycle. The same church with its wishing-well, a short cut straight to the past.

South of Rosebank, neighbouring Rondebosch is home to the University of Cape Town (UCT), handsomely festooned with creepers and sitting grandly on the mountainside

Map in hand, using UCT as my reference point, I scan for familiar street names, trying to remember where I spent – or, more accurately, squandered – four years of my life. Apart from Tugwell Hall, that pink monstrosity of the Seventies (that was a pink monstrosity even *in* the Seventies), I can no longer recall any of my former addresses. I drive at random, hoping for an epiphany, past seemingly identical blocks of flats, convinced, sequentially, that I lived in each of them. Or, no, in none. Somewhere else, then – on a map that no longer exists, in a bleak series of rented rooms, poky flats, and crumbling communal Victorians, where I cohabited with strangers. Like the ghosts that we are now, people came and went, some disappeared. We acquired the idiom of silence and paranoia. From time to time, a Special Branch man would be stationed outside a window, on a box, looking in.

If you get lost, a stranger may not be your best source of help

Somehow I find my way, on foot, up the hill to UCT. And now, at last, memory stirs, the part of me that is dead betrays, like a phantom limb, signs of life. Mounting the steps like a supplicant, as the grand neoclassical temple of Jameson Hall soars into view, just as it did when I first arrived, I re-experience – despite myself, despite everything – a surge of hope, an upwelling of possibility. I regain Jammie Steps, *once the seething heart of the struggle against apartheid;* it's like stepping into a digitally altered past. No banners, no tear gas, no drenching rain. Gradually, my eyes adjust. I recognise each building, though I've forgotten their names. I recognise the patch of lawn where we arty people used to sit. Arty people are sitting there still, digitally altered. The more I stare, the more I feel that nothing on campus has changed. Nothing, that is, except the student body. And that is everything.

The English Department, I discover, even *smells* the same.

Long Street is the main artery of Cape Town's cosmopolitan culture ... the most vibey part of Cape Town and the best place to have a good time

My Cape Town had no vibey zones, no cosmopolitan culture to speak of, except, perhaps, the occasional foreign film screened in some basement and the banned publications that circulated, dog-eared, from hand to hand.

Now, on Long Street or at the malls, in the vast flatland of cyberspace, you can buy any book in the world – if (big if) you can afford it.

I wander up and down Long Street, which strikes my jangled receptors as some kind of virtual reality, Global Ethnic Hipster World. A commodified Africa is on sale, with a brisk trade in beads and 'Whites Only' memorabilia. What I mainly notice are the street children. They remind me of the child who came to my door every morning for a year in Obs, barefoot, selling newspapers. I bought a paper, whether I wanted one or not, and gave him, every day, an orange. (An orange!)

Insider experiences:
Explore the dusty sprawl of a shanty town on a guided township tour

Against my better judgement, convinced somehow that *as a visitor to South Africa you need this eye-opener*, I take a group of students – New York students plus a few UCT classmates – on a township tour. Someone or Other's Cultural Tours, politically correct, I'm assured.

It's a failure. No, an unspeakable failure.

We visit Langa, Guguletu, Crossroads. We're in a giant air-conditioned coach, the approximate size of an ocean liner. The students are mortified, they stare at their laps. We disembark to inspect the living quarters of our fellow, less fortunate, human beings. The New York students from Guyana, Ecuador, and Bangladesh are underwhelmed; they wander outside after a cursory glance. *For travellers who've toured any other Third World hellhole, what you'll see here will come as little surprise.* The New York students from the suburbs and the 'hood are filled with a nameless disquiet that has something to do with shame but more with rage. They crowd into the bedroom of an affectless woman, our host, and avert their eyes. The Cape Town students, none of whom has ever set foot in the townships, grow very quiet. We put our cameras away. We play with the children, ply them with sweets. We pretend, afterwards, that it was a worthwhile expedition, though naturally not without its complications.

While the idea of a privileged international traveller voyaging through the poverty-stricken shanty towns of urban Cape Town may at first seem voyeuristic and insensitive –

You simply can't visit Cape Town and not experience the heart-warming communal love and cultural vibrancy that's abundant in our townships

Back on the muddy streets of Crossroads, a place I actually did visit in my do-gooding days, I'm struck by a single, traitorous thought: can so little really have changed? This is, after all, how millions live, not in the *elegant and tastefully restored* hostelries of the virtual Cape, *where a day on the beach meets a night on the town*. The only difference I can see is that the government no longer bulldozes the shacks on a regular basis.

This is the kind of thought I don't want to be having in the New South Africa. I censor it; I think, instead, about various types of power. I think about just who I think I am, standing here, having these thoughts.

I left South Africa because I didn't want to live in what then seemed a small, mean-spirited world, far away from everything. And now – perhaps deservedly – I do.

There was something pinched and impoverished about South African society then, an economy of emotional scarcity. But now, in almost all my encounters, I sense something open, alive, generous. Heliotropic. And the pinched, fearful mentality has migrated to the United States, producing, virus-like, its all-too-familiar symptomatology: Guantánamo, for instance, and the Patriot Act.

So I'm lost again and the guidebooks can't help me. Standing at Crossroads, I conduct a thought experiment. Could I, after half a lifetime half a world away, return? Return for real, I mean, find my way around without a map? Could I live here, work here, die here, in the actually existing place, not in some vanished Cape Town or some virtual Cape Town, not on some private Lonely Planet?

Clueless, I scan the Table of Contents like an Ouija board. There's a chapter I hadn't noticed before, *Customs*, which recommends a visit to a sangoma. The sangoma, it says, *will prescribe the correct muti for your condition*. Then I find the part that advises the reader *What to Say and*

How to Say It, and, finally, the paragraph on *Giving and Receiving*. *Cape Town is famed for its hospitality*, it assures me: the unannounced guest will never be refused. But if you're invited into a South African home, bring a gift – and remember that, in this country of ours, *Gifts are usually given and received with two hands*.

Jenefer Shute is the author of the novels *Life-Size*, *Sex Crimes*, *Free Fall*, and *User* ID, as well as numerous essays and articles. She was born in Johannesburg, studied at the University of Cape Town, and is currently a professor at Hunter College, New York, where she teaches in the MFA Programme in Creative Writing.

PR Anderson

On Common Ground

When I was a young boy returning from boarding school to Cape Town it was inevitably the mountain that I looked to for the first sure sign of home. It is the obvious landmark, obviously correlative for the security of roots, the solidity of family, the significance of parents. But the mountain is very far away to most of Cape Town. It rises up out of the sand flats and the sea, and from a distance it peters out in an enormous sky.

Up close, where I was white enough to live, the mountain had a different aspect to the famous table of the postcards. When rain kept the small boy at home for the whole of his holiday, he could stare out of the window at its hulk, towed into the roaring forties of the imagination like a battleship on its way to the breakers' yard. Then the mountain could be heard running with water, could be seen black with water through the cloud, could be smelt for its sodden forests. The boy me was always amazed that he should live in a city with forests within. The mountain still stands for home as soon as I see it through the bronze haze at the end of a journey, but it now stands for something else besides. It stands for what is unlikely about Cape Town.

There are any number of things odd about Cape Town, of the sort that only outsiders quite notice – like the way we have ornamented the lower slopes with wildebeest and zebras and deer, just fenced off from the motorway into town, across from the hospital. Or the way Bonnievale and Bonteheuwel are indistinguishable on the shouts of a taxi crier (though the Capetonian knows you will be going to Bonteheuwel). Nothing is so unlikely to me, though, as this wilderness at the centre of things, this national park and world heritage site, where you are never properly out of earshot of the thrumming city. I could not live in Cape Town without it (nor without the light of some afternoons, the scent of fish on a northwester, the rain). The spirit of a place is not anywhere particular, and in Cape Town it certainly is not in the national park. That common, defining Cape Town is in the elements of wind, sand, tar, salt, rail, rain – diffuse conditions that make sense to a Capetonian in their various combinations, just as they would to other citizens in their own cities. In truth, these things do not make sense, but are recognised, and are beloved in the degree to which, being recognised, they appear as reflections of ourselves. These things might be thought of as our likeness. We see ourselves in them and in the moods they induce. They stand for our likeness also in that we know – or believe – that others recognise themselves and us in them too. By contrast, the mountain, its forests, its dams and uplands, its paths of quartz sand, its clickety restios, its seeps, its stains, its lichens and rubbles, its carpenter bees, its porcupines, its now endemic fires, all these stand not for likeness, but for what is unlikely. The truth is that ours is not a mountain city, nor a city of forests (we are far more a city of sand flats). But we have a mountain, and the mountain has its forests.

The forests lie on the south-eastern face where the rain falls, and mark the frontier between the city and the mountain. They, like their mountain, are corrupted now. In the past they were logged for hardwoods for the shipyards in Cape Town and the wagoning out of Salt River. Then they were crowded with pine plantations, some of which persist. Now they are interrupted by vineyards, bluegum firebreaks, forestry roads, even some suburban development. But they remain, in all their versions, something somewhere between the city and the city's site. In this they do not quite belong to Cape Town, but are its threshold. That threshold lies between the present and the past, when once Cape Town was not. It lies between what we think of as civilisation and wilderness, categories that the forests themselves confound. It lies between the pre-colonial and the colonial place, and between the colonial place and what has come, or is coming, afterwards. It lies between what is corporate and public in the experience of Cape Town, and what is solitary and private.

*

I can still get lost in Newlands Forest, but it takes deep distraction or solid weather in the pine plantations. Now the plantations are all coming down, and thank God, to discover the contours under and before them, and new views. On the edges of the indigenous forest there is still the occasional ringbarked pine to be found through the fog, cross-hatched like a ham. The pines come down with an explosion, sodden and top-heavy in the onslaught of a cold front. Their detritus buries the long-lost paths: Ascension Hill Track, Marsley Track. On the main paths they are sawn up after a few days, and the ground is spattered with sawdust. But when an oak comes down it is properly dressed, being good timber. I saw four men struggling down alongside Newlands Stream with a three-metre plank that was almost a metre wide. They had slim hips and loose trousers, and one man had bundled his jacket for a pad on his shoulder. Their bodies were drunk under all that weight.

Even if the landmarks go, if you get lost there is always down, because the forest is on a mountainside.

Driving on the motorway that runs from the university through the posh suburbs to the south, I am always looking into the forest alongside and up to the mountain above it. On wintry days the retreating cloud paints Chinese watercolours of pinnacles and boughs, on summer days the air is so laden with dust and pollen that the great light seems particular, literally so, a kind of stuff. Then the mountain seems a matter of light so immense that the density of it presses in towards darkness, as if under the force of its own gravity.

Next to this the cars go by and the joggers jog in the fumes. There is a treaty of mutual disdain, between forest and city, that mostly holds.

Between the freeway and the trees lies a zone where the city engages the forest. There is the reservoir with its water still as a secret, the picnic site lost in the fatty smoke of Sunday afternoons, the helicopters that arrive with the swallows for a season of drought and wind and fires. The forest station under the plane trees boasts a never-changing number of accident-free days. Heavy vehicles come and go in the red and yellow of toys. Morning and afternoon the tannoy summons staff to a telephone, and a siren marks the knock-off. On hot days the air is painted with creosote. In spring you will find the odd snake crossing the tar. In autumn you will pass others returning with packets of mushrooms.

I do not love dogs, but I love the excitement of dogs at the forest station, where all their walks begin. Geese bray in unlikely roosts, canaries swizzle, sparrowhawks whistle in display, and at dusk the owls make noises of assent in the plantation above the reservoir.

Evenings, any day, are for the dogs and joggers. Sunday lunch propels the promenaders. Balloons in the car park announce a birthday party on some Saturdays. Frequently, but not regularly, you will smell dagga in the donga of Newlands Stream, and there on the mud see some small congregation of the earnest young, or more confident Rastafarians, with perhaps a drum. On weekdays, when the forest is empty, you will at some stage pass one or two young men walking fast, in overall trousers and shot T-shirts, smelling of mutton-fat and paraffin. They have a cloth bag and a purpose, which is to gather plants for the *muti* trade.

If you are a regular – and they are surprisingly few – then you will recognise this year's young lovers, the nonagenarian with the ski-stick, the bearded father with the son keen on owls, maybe now one and then the other of the bark-strippers, the economist with the ridgeback, the brute training for the Three Peaks, the woman with the old Peugeot and all the dogs, the retired-gents' walking club, where the one rule has evidently to do with the wearing of rugby socks – and yourself, too, for you will impress upon the forest your rounds and rituals.

I walk when the mushrooms come, one week after the first thronging rain of autumn, and loiter to pick them, but as much for the chipping of the frogs and the orange stain of the spores on my fingers. I walk with an umbrella in winter, in the kind of weather that only forsaken lovers walk in. I walk in spring when the keurbooms scent the scrub tracts like a sweet shop or a *kramat*. I walk in summer when the streams are dry across the contour path, and the forest is dry and dark as sleep.

It would be good to tell the story of what I find there, but what I am telling instead is about what is lost there, or, I should say, what I lose there. It is as commonplace of romantic sensibility to speak of losing oneself in contemplation, or nature, as it is to speak of finding oneself in the same. But I mean neither of those things of the forest. What I find there is the unlikely in my life. If I go to the forest, I enhance, as one might enhance a chance of something happening, the absurdity of my relation to the city, by which I mean the business of living in the human aggregate. That strangeness pulls the city and myself into a common focus, so that I can comprehend the place. It is an intuitive act, like walking without a fixed path, or perhaps writing. It suits me, the irony of having to go to the centre of the city to get out of it sufficiently to put myself back in it after all.

The things I list below are among the many losses and finds of the forest. They happen to no purpose, but at the unlikely centre of a substantial city. They are iterations of placement, perhaps as I am lost and found in each instance.

One Sunday afternoon I passed a boy stung by a bee that was maddened by his mother's ersatz scent. In its frenzy the hive swarmed on me. Bees appear black in numbers, tucked sting-in on you. I shed my clothes and ran for water, but there is no deep water in the forest. I had to have the bees whipped off me.

One midweek morning I walked alone in the forest and was followed everywhere by the breathing of a dog that was not there.

One Good Friday in Hiddingh Ravine I came upon three women scooping water from the stream where the path crosses it. They wore white robes and shawling cassocks of patchwork. Upstream a man with a painted face was

93

squatting on a rock. They half-sang in low voices among themselves and to nobody in particular. On the boulders of the stream was lit a circle of say thirty candles, floating their lights in the forest gloom. Above it all, grey southeaster weather, cloud about the summit of Hiddingh Buttress and the day's light, at noon, diffuse in the volume of dark invented by the mountain, the trees and the candles. Below it all, traffic thinned to a sigh by the public holiday, the sprawl of suburban dreck, single-storey Cape Town, the snoek-coloured bay, and the Kogelberg across it.

One morning, it could have been one of any day, I walked out of my office at the university, through the concourse of students, across the parking lot beneath the ruins of the old zoo, and into the forest. There are mornings when the forest leavens in the sunshine. The last of yesterday's heat is returned from the loam. Insects cast off like a blown dandelion. The whole thing ticks. I came down from the upper paths back towards my next lecture, making good time on the forestry road. I chose a transect that was both a short cut and one of those paths that are well drawn. I could hear the forestry station about its business below, and thought to skirt it. Ahead of me a red cat rose from its quilt of sunned earth. It was a lynx, a caracal. It was the cat Apollo, tuft-eared, sunburnt, stretching in the light. It saw me and trotted off down the path. I walked behind it, it trotted ahead, and then our ways diverged.

One year I set about finding the lost paths. There are several routes up to the contour path, but some have fallen into disuse or been suppressed. The old maps show them and give them names. I have found the closed paths easily enough. But there is one – Marsley Track – which has disappeared. It has been lost piecemeal. Some of it is now a section of a subsequent track, some of it is crossed by forestry road, some of it is obliterated in the timber of a felled plantation.

The fun lay in intuiting where the path must have led from its vanishing point. But the day came when there was no going forward. Marsley Track ended where the real forest began in a dark declivity, all mossed boulders and the wrack of past storms. I clambered about, nowhere in particular. For a moment I could hear nothing but myself thrashing in vines and thorns.

There is in that moment a knowledge that the path – the past – is truly lost, that no one has set foot where you do, or will ever know that you have. It came upon me as a kind of panic, the knowledge that I was lost. It was knowledge, not fact, for in the forest when the landmarks go there is always down. But in my panic I saw a wonderful thing: shaken from some foliage, in clouds about me, and settling on my hands, thousands and thousands of tiny whiteflies, both dry and damp at the same time, exactly like the ash of paper.

*

The forests are where I am alone in the city, and between it and the earth. Sometimes consciously, often unwittingly, this is why I go there – specifically to Newlands Forest, the forest closest to where I live and work, the forest closest to my childhood, the forest that grew on me as if in one night, where the wild things are, where I can think and stop thinking, where I am in the city and out of it altogether. In Newlands Forest I catch myself in the act of inhabiting, treading a space into the accommodation we know as place. In this it embodies all of our acts in shaping the Cape Town we inhabit, the Cape Town that is ours plurally and singly, that was once the place of those now dead and is now founded on them, a place about 34° S and 18° 30′ W, of which we have made that likeness which is of common ground, but where we live our own unlikely lives.

PR Anderson is a lecturer in the English Department of the University of Cape Town. His collection of poems, *Litany Bird*, appeared in 2000. A further collection is due to appear in the UCT Writers Series this year. His anthology of South African love poems, *In the Country of the Heart*, appeared in 2004.

Antony Sher

Playing Cape Town

'Welcome home Sir Antony – can I shake you by the hand?'

Over the last few days, I've received this greeting several times in Cape Town – I'm here to perform my one-man show, *Primo* – but never from someone like this. The man shaking my hand is a bergie: a bull-necked, dark-skinned character, maybe in his forties. I've often watched him from the balcony of the apartment which I'm renting in Bantry Bay. He lives on the boulders to the left of Saunders Rocks, and can be seen pacing back and forth along the front, searching through the blue bins on the railings: *Keep the Cape in Shape, Hou die Kaap in die Haak.* I'm surprised that he's recognised me, even more so that he seems well informed about my career. Later my friend, the theatre director Janice Honeyman, tells me that he's called Dassie, and that over the years she's also been impressed by his knowledge of current affairs and the arts. 'Maybe there are TV sets just out of view there,' she muses, gazing at the wall of rocks. 'Maybe the *Cape Times* is delivered daily.'

I was born and raised in Sea Point. In 1968 I left to attend drama school in London, and ended up settling there. My partner Greg and I fly back every year to see the family, who still live locally: Mom, my brothers Randall and Joel, my sister Verne, and their partners and children. But I've never, as the saying goes, played Cape Town. And what will it be like to live here again – for five weeks in January and February 2005? This is a big moment for me.

Shortly after my arrival, I have an experience which takes me right back to my earliest days. I'm asked to do a question-and-answer session in the hall of the Marais Road Shul. We used to live directly opposite, in a single-storey house with a sunny *stoep* in front and a large, rambling garden behind. It was knocked down some years ago, and a small, featureless block of flats put in its place. As I arrive at the shul tonight I find myself staring across the road with a peculiar feeling of anger: I can never visit that lovely house again, I can never see where I spent the first ten years of my life. The shul hall, on the other hand, is intact and familiar, though elusively so ... that musty, vaguely municipal scent, those glaring overhead lights, the slightly scuffed walls ... maybe we had cheder lessons here, maybe various shul functions. But I'm certainly clear about the last time I was here: it was the reception after my barmitzvah, forty-three years ago.

These days I'm a non-practising, non-believing Jew, so the welcome that tonight's packed audience give me is as surprising and touching as the one from Dassie. I begin by telling them about my barmitzvah. The whole event was traumatic. I'm tone deaf so I couldn't properly sing my portion of the Torah in the shul, and, as an intensely shy child, I also hated making my speech at the reception in this hall. When I left on that day in 1962, I remember thinking: I got through it, and I'll never have to perform in public again. And here I am now in 2005, doing a one-man show for God's sake.

Although I've lived in England much longer than I ever lived in Cape Town, sense memories are waiting to ambush me round every corner. They induce a haunting feeling, a kind of ache. Not because they're unpleasant – quite the opposite – it's just that the past is so long ago it seems incredible that the present still looks and feels the same. The blast of air as I open the sliding doors in my apartment each morning, that Sea Point air, flavoured with ocean water and kelp. Or the way the afternoon sunlight lies, baking and still, on a neighbour's yard – on the frangipani tree, the deckchair, the old whitewashed walls, everything slightly dusted with sea salt. Or the hot, steep roads up to Fresnaye smoking after a brief rainstorm. Or the day I wake up to what looks like winter: drizzle, mist, and Lion's Head decapitated.

Other aspects of my home town strike me like they might a first-time visitor. Table Mountain is impossibly beautiful, impossibly huge, impossibly near: how can one live in such proximity to a giant? Every day as I'm driven to the Baxter Theatre, where I'm doing *Primo*, the mountain takes my breath away, every single day. I try to have a siesta during these journeys – the rush-hour traffic makes them long and slow – and so I view the spectacle half asleep, half awake, and maybe that's appropriate: it's a mountain from a dream, and the dream was my childhood. Chapman's Peak and Noordhoek, which I visit on days off, make a similar impact. They're both giants too – a giant coastal view, a giant beach – and I have to constantly pinch myself: did I really grow up alongside these phenomenal places? Were they ever ordinary? Because I honestly can't remember noticing them much back then. Imagine not noticing Table Mountain. How can that be?

I suppose it's because I felt out of place. And so I never

properly occupied my place, Cape Town, I never properly took it in. We often talk of feeling 'out of place', but for me it held real meaning during my adolescence. I was drawn to the arts while most of the other boys at Sea Point High seemed more interested in sport; and I was drawn to those boys too, while they were more interested in the girls at Ellerslie. Being Jewish didn't feel particularly popular or safe either. Nothing was comfortable, nothing seemed to fit. Looking back now, I wonder if my feelings of unease within my society, a sense of it being brutal and threatening, wasn't also to do with the fact that it was wrong, morally wrong. I couldn't have articulated this at the time – I didn't develop any political awareness till I reached London – but I don't believe you can belong to a system as violent and perverse as apartheid, even if you're part of the ruling class, and not be disturbed by it on some deep level. You *know* it isn't right, you *know* human beings aren't meant to live like this.

Back in the Sixties all I wanted to do was leave Cape Town. These days, I can't wait to come back. It isn't just that I rejoice in South Africa's flourishing democracy; it's also because those childhood impressions of my birthplace are imbedded in me, even if I was rather careless collecting them in the first place. The sense memories are like seeds: they lie dormant in me for most of the year while I'm in the UK, but I only have to step off the plane at Cape Town International Airport, and the sunlight only has to hit them, and a plunge in the sea only has to water them, and they blossom again, and their fragrance breaks my heart.

Alongside familiar things, others are new. Including the Baxter itself. The theatres I remember from my youth were the Hofmeyr, the Labia, and Maynardville. But now the Baxter is the one that everybody talks about. It seems that Mannie Manim has done for Cape Town what he did for Joburg in 1976 when he co-founded the Market

Theatre with Barney Simon: creating a theatre that speaks excitingly to the people, all the people. When you work in this business, you only have to step into a theatre building to know whether it's alive and well. The buzz in the Baxter is palpable. Both shows in the other auditoria are playing to packed houses – *Kat and the Kings* and *Joe Barber 3* – and I'm intrigued to see how Coloured these audiences are. (Are you still allowed to say 'Coloured'? The only thing I don't like about the New South Africa is the endless political correctness. As a moffie Jew-boy whitey I protest!) Before *Primo* opens I'm warned by the Baxter people that it might not be as full as the other shows – it might be too serious, particularly at this time of year – but they're proved wrong, and they celebrate this as much as I do.

From the Baxter audiences to the newspaper coverage, from the bergie Dassie to the Marais Road Shul congregation, my welcome home in Cape Town is completely bloody wonderful. It includes an evening I will never forget.

Primo is my adaptation of Primo Levi's book *If This is a Man*, in which he describes his incarceration in Auschwitz in 1944. Without making any glib comparisons between the Holocaust and apartheid, I'm nevertheless aware that certain lines in the piece resonate here in South Africa with extra force. Early on in the piece, Primo, an Italian Jew, talks of 'the life of segregation forced on me by the racial laws'. Later, commenting on one of his German oppressors in Auschwitz, he says, 'When I was free again, I wanted to meet him – not out of revenge, just curiosity.' Is that Primo Levi talking or Albie Sachs? Every performance in the Baxter's tiny studio theatre is charged, but on 27 January this charge is so strong it touches me to my core. The date is the sixtieth anniversary of the liberation of Auschwitz by the Russian army in 1945. All round the world there are ceremonies commemorating that historic moment. Here in Cape Town, a specially invited audience comes to *Primo*, including several Holocaust survivors, the Italian and the British consuls, and also Ebrahim Rasool and Desmond Tutu. The moment in the story when Primo announces the date and then describes the Russians arriving is more powerful than anything I've ever felt in the theatre. In fact it isn't theatre – it's something beyond, something else. I feel so moved, so proud that it's happening here in Cape Town, back at home.

The family had already seen the show by then; they came on the opening night, even Mom. She's ill these days, with Alzheimer's – although, mercifully, she has a peaceful form of the disease. She just wants to stay at home all the time. During my stay, I resolve to lunch with her every day and contribute, in a small way, to all the devotion my siblings have shown her in recent years. They've enabled her to stay on in the family house in Alexander Road, looked after by a full-time carer, a large, cheerful Afrikaner, Gail Junge, and part-time by Katie Roberts, who has worked as Mom's cook for well over half a century. Katie herself is in her eighties now, and not as robust as she was, yet still makes the long journey from Bonteheuwel three times a week to cook favourite dishes for Mom, and now me: tomato bredie, green-bean stew, and, most specially, 'Katie's bagels'. These are not like the deli bagels, which just tend to be soft buns with holes in them; these are very crisp outside, with a shallow doughy centre, uniquely delicious. Katie learned the recipe from Mom's mom, who learned it from her mom, who learned it back in the tiny *shtetl* of Plungyan in Lithuania, before emigrating to South Africa. How many different stories are in this Cape Town house each lunchtime, I think to myself. Mom, once a strong Sea Point Jewish matriarch, now frail of body and vague of mind, attended to by an elderly Coloured lady who can bake genuine Lithuanian bagels, and a chatty Afrikaner *vrou*, who tells me that some

102

of her female ancestors perished in the concentration camps invented by the British during the Boer War. And here's me, a Brit myself now, playing an Italian concentration-camp survivor.

Occasionally Mom and I lunch just on our own. The dining room is shadowy – Mom likes the blinds drawn, and complains about the heat – and the atmosphere is particular: quiet, restrained, sad-sweet. Mom rarely initiates conversations, or if she does, it's a repeat of something she's just asked me. So I do the best I can, telling her stories about last year in the UK or last night at the Baxter. Sometimes it's like the old days – she's engaged and amused – and sometimes it's simply hard work. Distressingly, it's lodged in her mind that I'll be going back to London one of these days, but she can't quite remember when it is. So she constantly enquires, 'Is it today – the day of the airport?' slightly spoiling all the precious time we do have together.

About halfway through my stay, I develop a new ritual: jumping off Big Rock into the sea at Saunders. We all used to do this as kids, but I was apprehensive about trying it now. Bullied by Janice Honeyman, who is a keen and regular jumper, I finally have a go, and then finally became hooked on it, indulging at least twice a day. Leaping into the icy Atlantic sends an exquisite shock through the system, every fibre of the body, even the brain. It's certainly the best cure for a hangover I've ever known. Janice, who has just flown in from the States, says it even cures jet lag.

I become intrigued by the beach population here. In my youth it was whites-only of course, and my abiding memory is of a crowd of elderly, retired Jewish gents lounging on the rocks, yattering loudly about nothing at all. The same age group, doing the same thing, is still here, except they now yatter in Afrikaans, and they're all Malay. I go down for my afternoon jump off Big Rock at about four o'clock, and this is when I regularly meet Dassie, and he quizzes me about the state of the British film industry or what it's like to be knighted. Gradually the old boys on the beach also get to know me, and we all raise a lazy hand and mumble, 'Hi.' The most senior of the group, a large-boned, bald chap in red trunks, fascinates me. It's the way he relishes the sunshine on these rocks, sprawling luxuriously, almost purring with pleasure – it's like he's catching up on all those years when he wasn't allowed here.

On the morning of my last full day, the last Sunday of *Primo*'s run, a miracle occurs. I'm chatting on the phone to my brother Randall when I glance out the window. Just beyond Saunders Rocks, I see a fin in the water, then a tail, now a plume of misty water. I hurry to my balcony. Everywhere you look, the sea is full of whales: blowing, diving, rolling, some breaching. But surely this is impossible? Surely by now (early February) they should be feeding in the Antarctic? Don't they only return to these shores, mainly at Hermanus, to breed in September, October? Maybe they've sussed that the long, gruelling migration to the South Pole isn't worth it any more, and they might as well just party in Cape Town through the summer like everyone else. Or maybe, as Greg says when I ring him in London, 'They've come to say goodbye to you.' Greg and I are wildlife fanatics, and have had tremendous visits to Hermanus during the whale season, and to Cape Ann in Massachusetts, where the viewing is also exceptional.

Whale-watching makes any other activity difficult. This morning I cut myself shaving, trying to look in the mirror and out of the window at the same time. I am also trying to finish a piece of writing before I go in for the matinee, but I expect when I revise it tomorrow it'll read: 'abooglybonglewyzx'. It's agony leaving for work. Eventually the driver, Wilhelm, has to force me into the car. I insist we take the Beach Road route. Everywhere people are lined along the railings, gazing out to sea, hushed with wonder. They look like a religious congregation.

The following morning, the whales are gone from my view: vanished as mysteriously as they appeared. This final Sunday passes in a blur – a family braai, lots of upsetting goodbyes – and then, just before I'm due to leave, Randall suggests one last jump off Big Rock. He drives me back to Saunders. As we leap into the sea, I feel that special jolt go through me, that sense of total cleansing, and try to hold onto the sensation, aware that that it will be at least a year before I can do this again.

Climbing the steps up to Beach Road, I suddenly realise that I haven't seen my pal Dassie today. I wanted to give him a gift, and to say goodbye. This feels important. I search up and down, but no luck. Then, just when Randall says we really must go, I finally spot Dassie lying in the shade of a tree. As we shake hands, he must think it strange that my voice is breaking and my eyes are full. There's a final, tougher farewell ahead for me, with Mom – today *is* the day of the airport – but somehow more than anyone else it's Dassie, with his unexpected and informed interest in me, who has symbolised my stay here over the past five weeks. Playing Cape Town has turned out to be one of the most remarkable moments of my career, and of my life.

Antony Sher, the actor and writer, was born in 1949 and raised in South Africa before going to London to study at the Webber Douglas Academy of Dramatic Art. After performing for the theatre group Gay Sweatshop in T*hinking Straight* (1975), T*he Fork* (1976) and S*tone* (1976), Sher joined the Royal Shakespeare Company in 1982. Three years later, his performance in the title role of R*ichard* III won him an Olivier

Award for Best Actor, and in 1997 he won another Olivier Award for *Stanley*. Although he spends more time acting in the theatre, Sir Antony has also appeared in a number of films and TV series, including *The History Man* (1981), *Shadey* (1985), *The Young Poisoner's Handbook* (1995), *The Wind in the Willows* (1996), *Mrs Brown* (1997) and *Shakespeare in Love* (1998).

Sindiwe Magona

Home

The dark cloud that hung over our family suddenly burst a bright, bright streak and my little heart leapt to my throat. We were going to Cape Town! My brother and I were going to Cape Town! This startling piece of news hit me shortly after the death of our maternal grandmother, Mamkwayi, with whom we were living.

Months before, Mother had taken ill and gone to Cape Town, where Father worked and where better medical facilities existed. My brother and I, the two older children, were left in the care of her parents. Mama took baby Siziwe with her. But now, her mother had died; and Father was coming to take us to Cape Town. The thought that *I* was going to that big, faraway place filled me with such excitement as would be hard to imagine.

Visions of a grandeur I had no knowledge of, had never seen, assaulted me. A brick house with windows of glass. Electricity instead of candles and the infernal rag-and-can paraffin lamp. Water – not from the river but spouting right out of the inside walls of the very house in which I live – what magnificence! What splendour! No princess ever felt grander than little me during those days of shivery anticipation.

Upon my arrival, however, the big city revealed itself as anything but glamorous. My Cape Town turned out to be a small, dark, damp room at the back of another family's shack in a subsection of Blouvlei called 'Forest', perhaps in sad recall of some faraway time when trees still lived in that now barren and dune-dotted landscape of tired sand and sad scrub.

Sand. Sand. Sand. And everywhere and all around, sand. That was Blouvlei. The place didn't even have an excuse for a street or road, tar or otherwise. No one had thought to plan the location or, events having overtaken city planning, upgrade it. What was there was what nature had given, tempered by the passage of time and the rapaciousness of man. There were hills, and there were flats. But the dominant feature of Blouvlei was the sand: bright-white, blinding-to-the-eye at the hilltops; and at the lows or flats, dull, dirty, almost black from all the trampling in an area with no waste-disposal services – and any number of shades you care to guess in between these two extremes. But that terrain, well known, beloved, dangerous, was my playground. That is where we children ran and ran and ran – with never a fence to bar our way. And although more often than not broken glass gashed our feet, with no thought of doctor, nurse, or Dettol, we daily abandoned ourselves to carefree play.

Blouvlei was vast – a sprawling sea of shacks – as far as the eye could see. KwaSolomon, eForest, KwaSmith and KwaKrismesi – those are the sections of Blouvlei I remember now. After eForest, we moved KwaSolomon. But the futile search for a better or bigger shack soon had us return eForest.

It was a hard, hard childhood. But we children knew little of that hardship for we were all similarly afflicted. If everyone you know feasts on tripe, you're hardly likely to be yearning for T-bone steak. And if all your playmates are in various stages of tatteredness, who can laugh at whose rags?

I started school in Blouvlei, in a one-room shack in which two classes were held at the same time. Not one of those children ever wore a shoe to school. Very few had even one item of the uniform – to say nothing of any child turning up in full uniform. *The complete regalia?* Who'd ever seen such a miracle in Blouvlei? I lived in Blouvlei, so I went to school in Blouvlei. That is how it was done back then, a child went to school where that child lived – unless one had parents of means. Then one was sent to boarding school, out in the Transkei or Ciskei or, indeed, another province – anywhere but the Western Cape, the country's Coloured Preferential Area. Sundays, we went to church. The service was held in a tiny, one-room affair, a shack. So was the shop – a shack. Tatomkhulu Mavuthengatshi, Dora Tamana's older brother, owned the only shop Blouvlei boasted – something like your corner convenience store. For grander shopping, we went to the Indian and Chinese shops along Retreat Main Road. Blouvlei was part of Retreat; or so it believed. But now, when a friend looks up the place in an old map of Cape Town, she can't find Blouvlei. Lost? Forgotten? I know it is no imaginary place. I know it existed once. I know because I lived there.

Our last house eForest was in one of those structures we called 'buildings'. A building was a row of several attached houses. The building in which we lived was one of the more ambitious schemes. There must have been anything from fifteen to twenty houses in each of the double rows facing each other so that we had something of a courtyard, if no paving. Well, one *shushu* day, a Primus stove exploded in one of those houses and, with the speed of a straw fire on bonfire day, the whole edifice burned to the ground.

Enter the Cape Town City Council. Now and then the local authority would find it expedient to perform some task, acknowledging the existence of some of its voiceless, voteless citizens. New Site Location was such a grand gesture. A shack fire, then as now, provided good mileage for the ambitious politician. Someone must have presented a very strong case regarding the plight of the victims of that fire. However, if you think the solution entailed something different, think again. The CCC gave a piece of land to the fire victims. And here, 'give' is not quite appropriate; do not overestimate the generosity of the CCC. Africans had no right to immovable property. The families were allowed to pitch new shacks on the plot but they would never own the land. But this was the first time my father had built his own house to his own design – Kwazwelitsha! Our parents had their own bedroom – another first!

We had lost Siziwe KwaSolomon. Our brother, Mawethu, was born eForest, a few years later. When we came Kwazwelitsha, the family had three children. Ten years later, uprooted by the government's forced removals, we still had the same house; it still had its two bedrooms. Meanwhile, we had three more children; and big brother and I were now in our serious teens.

As an African child, my Cape Town was vastly different to the Cape Town of those of my differently classified compatriots. But just as my eyes, like all eyes, could feast freely on the mountain and the sea – the sea and the mountain – my spirit chose to dwell not on what man gives or withholds but what my Cape Town, my generous Mother, freely gives – not only the sea and the mountain but the fire and ice the place burns and etches into the souls of those who live in this city or merely pass through its open gates. Who could pass by the majesty and splendour of Cape Town and not be inspired to humaneness by its sheer natural beauty?

And so, from that poverty-ridden childhood, I remember parents who showered me with love and security; when the words 'I love you' were never so much as uttered; when sparing the rod was out of the question; and when hunger loomed, menacing daily. But the whole Blouvlei 'village' held me in the palm of its communal hand. I remember playmates, many of whom were sentenced to early graves by poverty, and I am saddened. I am grateful for fathers and big brothers who kept me safe and taught me respect for self and others. I have fond memories of mothers who fed me when hungry; who did not hesitate to pull me by the ear when I fell short of expected standards of behaviour. In my inner ear, the sounds of my childhood still ring: the Saturday drum of what we knew then as 'sects' – *ooSigxabhayi* and *amaZiyoni*; or the witchdoctors' drums that thudded from Friday afternoon till Sunday morning, when the 'Great Ones' would come out and perform their 'Thanksgiving' dance-prayer before dispersing. Oh, the frenzy of those dances – both the religious and the traditional! The brilliance of attire! The unrestrained hollers and the burning lyrics – how could one escape believing?

Just as irresistible, as vibrant, as colourful, was that once-a-year event, the *Klopse* – the Cape Coon Carnival that followed hard on the heels of Cafda's Christmas party. At the latter, we got toys and ate pies, ice cream and other 'frivolous' fare we never saw in our solidly *'stamp en stoot'* homes.

As the child of economic migrants, augmenting the

family income was a necessity I grasped from very early on. The vineyards of Tokai and Constantia know me, for my feet have followed their pathways in search of after-harvest gleanings. I am grateful to the farmer, to his wife, and to his child that I was allowed to roam his fields and knit colourful memories of my childhood – a giving childhood. I choose to remember the kindness because that was my experience then. I defy the jaundiced eye of the grown-up me, the hoarse whisper of regret, anger, and resentment that would tarnish this memory with whispers of politically correct, self-righteous chagrin. Allowing such revision would deprive me of something more precious than gold – memories of a happy childhood – memories that have swayed me to return to this place, this temptress without equal, this mother whose bounteous breast feeds so many but remains ever flowing: my Cape Town.

But the Cape Town of my memory also belongs to apartheid South Africa. And if the apartheid laws of the country dehumanised all Africans (as they were meant to), nowhere was this more stringently observed than in the Western Cape, which was proclaimed a Coloured Preferential Area. Among other things, an African could not be hired until Coloured Affairs stated that no Coloured person wanted that position. This was above and beyond the jobs Africans were barred, by law, from doing. I was in my teens before Golden Arrow hired the first crop of African bus drivers. Also, Africans could only undergo any form of professional training in the Transkei, the Ciskei, or other provinces – but not in the Western Cape. That is why, when the time came for me to study to become a teacher, I had to leave Cape Town.

My Cape Town therefore was a place of forbidden fruit, where all things good were out of reach: NO PERSON UNDER 19, NO DOGS, and NO BANTU the cinemas of Cape Town boasted, barring me entry, as did the safe beaches, the good schools, the posh residential areas. Some sages even suggested different shopping days for the likes of me. They spoke of jumbo-jetting migrant workers on a daily basis from the villages to the cities and farms that needed their labour but loathed the bodies to which the hands that performed that labour were attached. Of course, if Africans were not welcome in places of worship, in restaurants, on the beach, in residential areas, in schools, or at the graveyard, it stands to reason they were far from welcome in places of employment – that citadel of capitalist competitiveness. The 'Wanted' ads then still read: 'Fair-skinned Coloured girl …'

For four years after I'd lost my teaching job, I could not find employment. What with the job reservation laws excluding me from many jobs, plain racial discrimination from still others, I resorted to that mecca of African women, domestic work. Now, there is nothing wrong with any kind of employment, including domestic work. But there is everything wrong with a system that sentences one race to perpetual servitude. No family should see three generations of its women slave their lives away in menial work. Yes, I know, these women need the jobs. But shouldn't these same jobs pay them enough to save their daughters from the drudgery suffered by the mothers? Make no mistake, domestic work is hell. If it were anything but, I bet you that white women and men of all races would long have found a way to take it away from the African woman. The innovation some employers are capable of is amazing. One woman needed a sleep-in maid. I needed a job as a matter of utmost urgency. This Wetton *medem* hired me although she had no accommodation. I slept in the garage. Yes, with her car in the garage.

Yet, despite woundings untold, I have returned. I have returned for I could not do otherwise. While on vacation, two years before retirement (as part of the exercise of

113

'making up my mind' whether to apply for a Green Card or take the Repatriation – two options the United Nations offered), I asked a friend to drive me to Retreat, to the area that used to be home. I knew our shack-home would not be there, bulldozed with my family watching, helpless decades ago. But ... surely ... something ... anything ... would be recognisable.

Klip; Busy Corner; Main Road, Retreat; Twelfth Avenue; Eleventh Avenue; Sixth Avenue!

Time reels back.

'Happy Home!' The Ngozi family! Mankunku, Nomangesi and Stoshana live here!

Happy Home – KwaTshawe! KwaMam' uMangwanya!

'Turn back,' a voice croaks.

'Are you okay?' Jeff asks, careful not to look my way.

'I'm fine.'

He nods, turns around and silently drives on. Does he know? Does he even suspect? A burning anger has seized me. I am mad. So sad. Devastated.

My father, dead these thirty years and more. What was it like to be him? What was it like to be so emasculated by the apartheid regime? What was it like to be a man who had absolutely no say in the way his own life would be lived? Not even in choosing the house where his family would live? To have no say in where that house would be? *Tata!* What wretched wounding you suffered! How helpless – utterly helpless – you felt! How humiliating! Even birds build nests in trees of their choosing. Wild animals live where they choose.

This minute, how I suffer for my father, *with* my father; understand more clearly yet another aspect of his suffering; suffer as I have only once before suffered for him – on his passing.

But I grew into womanhood in this place. My two

daughters were born at Somerset Hospital, Green Point. It is there that I first became a mother. Groote Schuur Hospital – what bitter-sweet memories you evoke in me! My only son was born there. There, almost thirty years apart, both my parents died. Naturally, I am grateful for the care you gave them; but still you are the place to which I lost my parents; and my mother, her only sister, Legina Mabandla, a nursing sister at the Dr Stals Sanatorium, Westlake.

Clearly, when I was a child, Cape Town hardly showed me her gentler side. How is it then that having spent more than half my working life in New York, I chose to return to this city upon retirement? How is it that, with the memory of an indelible wounding in my heart, in my soul, I returned to her, hope once again knocking against my ribcage, assuring me of Cape Town's boundless possibilities, her generosity of spirit, her infinite physical beauty, and her rightness for me?

Back in the days when Afrikaans was a dirty word and learning it tantamount to the 'biter bit', I was forced to read a short story whose title and author I no longer recall. What struck me then, and has stayed with me since, is the ending of that story, an ending decrying the profanity of 'progress' that blights the natural majesty of place; such as the sacrilege shown in building ''n lelike ou huisie' right at the top of Table Mountain. Man's achievement, his pride in his 'conquest' of nature: what is it compared to what he found there – waiting, welcoming, freely given? Imagine my anger and consternation as I watch ugly building after ugly building go up against the beautiful, majestic giant's very flanks. How can we allow such desecration? What will we bequeath posterity?

Of all the places where I have gone I have regarded none as home – none but this city, this place, this Cape Town, where some savage long ago stopped a moment, arrested his plundering urges and described it as 'the fairest cape in the whole circumference of the earth'. That is Cape Town – was

Cape Town – before the onslaught of civilisation, modernity, and progress; before greed and creed encroached. That is Cape Town – still dazzling. Magnificent. Awesome.

Yes, no doubt, the sea and the mountain beckoned. But my return signalled no answer to some call of the wild; at least, that certainly was not the complete, not the only answer. Something deeper, primeval even, pulled and tugged at my heartstrings.

'*Inkaba yakho iyakulilela!* Your umbilical cord cries out for you!' amaXhosa say to explain the urge that is not to be denied – the homing instinct. The umbilical cord, buried deep in the ground after the birth of a child, marks 'home'. And the belief is that this place has a pull on one.

My umbilical chord is buried eGungululu, a village in Tsolo, near Umtata. But I grew up in Cape Town. I have lived here much of my life. My rites of passage and most of the significant events in my life took place here. And, above all, it is here that first our sister, born directly after me (*endamshiyela ibele*), then Mama's only sister, Aunt Legina, and, lastly, my parents are buried. Sadly, we lost the first two graves to poverty and forced removals. But the bones in all these graves have called and I have returned. Bone calling bone; just as, one day, I shall return to the earth from whence I came; dust to dust. Now, I see, I may have chosen the place of my burial – this city, my Cape Town!

Sindiwe Magona lives in Cape Town. She is the author of *To My Children's Children* and *Mother To Mother*.

André Brink

Persistence of Memory

A letter to K

Your question was very simple: *Why Cape Town?* The answer is unexpectedly more complicated. A love that can be explained is not love. In this case it involves lifetimes. My own, to start with. But the whole biography of a town as well, from its infancy, with flocks of fat-tailed sheep and herds of long-horned cattle grazing along the lower slopes of Table Mountain tended by their Khoi herders, to the aggressive signs of early middle age in today's vista of skyscrapers, freeways and flyovers (one abruptly halted in mid-flight), billboards, traffic snarls, concrete aspirations, failures – and, admittedly, a few rare successes – of the architectural imagination, hospitals like malignant growths, the brown clouds of urban pollution.

Why, indeed, Cape Town? I have often told you – in response to your memories of Poland, escape into exile, meanderings in Austria, the United States, Wales, and Austria again – about growing up in seemingly placid but inwardly seething little villages in the deep interior (the Free State, Griqualand West, the Eastern Transvaal), pursuing the nomadic lifestyle of ancestors probing the ever-receding limits and frontiers of a wide new land. Nothing about a Mother City brooding like a hen at the southern tip of our brown continent.

And yet it has been there in the background of my life all the time. For at the start of the summer holidays every year, we would pile into my father's grey 1938 Hudson and head south. When my friend Christie went on this same trip with his family – which included three boys – their father would stop after every hundred miles and give each of the three boys a hiding: even if they hadn't been unruly he knew that punishment would be appropriate soon. My father was more long-suffering: we only stopped to pee or picnic, including hot coffee from a flask smelling of tea, and cold water smelling of the canvas of the bag draped over the radiator. For two days, sometimes three, we would mark our grim progress across the plains and ridges of the interior followed by billowing clouds of dust, until we would draw up on the last rise below the Boland mountains to behold the sprawl of the city wedged between its two dark-blue oceans and know that we had, again, arrived. This was the single unwavering point of reference of my youth. A place of holiday, of blustering wind and blistering sunshine, of fighting with male cousins and falling in love – at a very safe distance – with their sisters (nut-brown Annatjie, black-haired Stella, freckled Miemie), of story-telling uncles and cushioned aunts, of fruit and grapes and the taste of Oom Jannie's forbidden wine, of shopping in towering places with staircases that moved magically by themselves, of consuming ice cream and pancakes in the Koffiehuis, meeting strange strangers known only to one's parents at Fletcher & Cartwright's, or feeding squirrels in the Company Gardens, or taking cable car rides up to the portals of Heaven, or swimming in the dark-blue ice-cold seas of Melkbos (my Great-Aunt Anna in her nightdress billowing hugely around her in the churning water). A world so far from the space in which we lived inland that it seemed as foreign and imaginary as Jerusalem or Gomorrah or Baghdad from the stories of the Bible and Scheherazade which were my staple diet.

Around me, places changed all the time, each merging disconcertingly into the others: Vrede, Jagersfontein, Brits, Douglas, Sabie, Lydenburg, Potchefstroom, Bothaville. New people, new friends, new teachers, new schools, new everything, every four years or so. But behind all this there remained that one constant to which we could return and acknowledge as a surrogate home at the end of every endless year. Cape Town.

The first time this became part of my consciousness (because in my childhood and youth it was merely part of the unexamined life) was in late July 1961, when my wife Estelle and I arrived in Table Bay on the Something Castle (Warwick? Edinburgh? Windsor?). The previous two weeks at sea, in grey weather, the great majority of the grey passengers had spent in the smoking rooms smoking. But in the early hours of that morning, there appeared a streak of lurid red in the sky, as if some great hand had taken up a red pencil to score out the erroneous writing of the immediate past and turn the page to start again. On this page was gradually inscribed the ink-black mass of the mountain above the ink-blue wash of the sea; and as the ship drew nearer and the sky became luminous, the sprawling city assumed a recognisable shape under tumbling gulls. One of those incomparable winter days when the rain clouds dissipate to reveal, in blue and gold, the sight that had already struck dumb Sir Francis Drake, as it must have Diaz and Vasco da Gama before him, and who knows, millennia earlier, Phoenicians on their way to unimaginable new worlds. Before our eyes the picture came to life. And then the Capeness of the Cape exploded in my ears with the trumpet voices of 'Coloured' harbour workers gleefully coaxing us ashore. 'Jus' look at these pale *outjies* coming down the gangway!' shouted one to a distant friend. 'White like *blerrie* maggots. *Aitsa*! Bring on that sun to give them a spot of colour, man.'

Aitsa: the exclamation derived from the once-hallowed name of Heitsi-Eibib, hunter-god of the Khoi people.

That was when I knew, with a recognition so fierce it took my breath away, that I had indeed come home. *Home*, a concept I had never grasped so acutely before: not during the previous years of studying in Paris, nor in that string of villages in the dusty heart of the country where one never dared grow too fond of anything or anyone, as goodbye was always in the air. Rilke: *These things that live on departure*. But this, now, suddenly, was *home*.

I was heading inland; I had already accepted an appointment at Rhodes University in Grahamstown. But *this* was home. This was where I wanted to be.

It took thirty years before I could take the step. But when I finally made the definitive move in 1991 when the University of Cape Town found a place for me, it was like entering more deeply into myself. There was nowhere else I could so naturally, so inevitably, be at home.

And its defining component was those exuberant early-morning voices, spoken or yelled by those people who are still not granted the dignity of their own name. Not even Coloureds, but '*so-called* Coloureds'. A people that began to emerge about nine months after the arrival of the first Dutch colonists. Who brought with them a flag of the Dutch

East India Company, the VOC; and a variety of dialects; and a very basic, fundamentalist brand of Calvinism; to plant a garden for the provisioning of passing ships, and tame the fringes of a rude interior (cordoned off, initially, by a hedge of bitter wild almond trees, then by mud walls, later by the stone walls of a little fort), and introduce the ball-game of miscegenation. Nothing homogeneous about the new generation of Cape inhabitants then generally known as 'Afrikaners', except perhaps the many shades of brown that separate black and white. And, surprisingly soon, their language. In this peculiar melting pot indigenous peoples and imported slaves (from Indonesia and Malaysia, from Malabar and Madagascar and Mozambique, from Amboine and Angola) attempting to speak the master language, Dutch, transformed it into something new, a local fabrication, soon known as *Afrikaans*. Which for a century and a half marked the speakers as locals, an underclass, largely of half-breeds, speaking a patois derided as Kitchen Dutch.

Yet it was the Western Cape, with Cape Town as its hub, where the Coloured people found their most authentic home. This, above all, was what defined that homecoming in 1961. And not long afterwards I had the joy of being introduced to the very heart of the Coloured Cape, District Six. By then, the ruthless bulldozers of the apartheid regime had already begun to lay waste the lower slopes of the mountain where The Six had teemed and pullulated for centuries. But there were still swathes of the old community left, and my friend Daantjie Saayman would take me on long walks through the once vibrant quarter which would later be the heart of *Looking on Darkness* and of much of *The Wall of the Plague*. (Daantjie himself was to become the model for the protagonist Andrea's larger-than-life fisherman father. Long before colon cancer finally struck Daantjie down.) This, like the Malay Quarter on the slope of the Lion's Rump, is what truly spells Cape Town for me: its indomitable, raucous, rebellious way of saying *No* – not only to apartheid, but to everything that tried to domesticate and inhibit the human spirit and its wild, affirmative freedom, its laughter, its compassion. And also its outrageous and jubilant way of saying *Yes* – to life itself, without inhibition or shame or reservation. A *Yes* all the more remarkable for the long darkness it had to traverse in order to return to the sun.

Much of that darkness – the darkness that lends relief and contours to the emotional and moral landscape of the Cape – was defined by slavery. For many years white historians lulled us with assurances of a relatively benign dispensation affecting slaves at the Cape, from the arrival of the first men, women and children in bondage in 1658 until the abolition of the barbaric practice in 1834. We know today that the experience was both more violent and more widespread, and assumed many more forms, than used to be believed. And Cape Town was at the heart of the system. Punishment ranged from the 'mild practices' involving the cutting off of noses, ears or heels to the lingering agony (sometimes protracted for six or eight or twelve days) of being left to die on the wheel after having all the limbs of the body shattered, or of being impaled on a long pole thrust up the anus and protruding through the neck, or drawn and quartered by four horses attached to the arms and legs of the condemned.

Here was the punishment meted out to the young woman Trijntje of Madagascar in 1714, when it came to light that she had been forced into a relationship with the brewer Willem Menssink (a violent man who used to thrash his own wife Elizabeth into submission exclaiming, 'Don't you know that it is the Cape custom to live by the Old Testament?'). Driven to despair by the violent advances of the brewer and the cruelty of his wife, Trijntje attempted to poison her mistress, and murdered the child Menssink had fathered on her. For this, she was taken to the place of execution at the south-eastern corner of the Castle, strangled to death, and her body tied to a forked post where it was left 'to be consumed by time and the birds of heaven'. (Menssink, of course, being white, and indispensable in supplying beer to the Company, went scot free.)*

This story was researched by the indefatigable Nigel Penn and published in his scintillating study, *Rogues, Rebels and Runaways* (1999); and I still remember the little smile with which he offered me the book, saying, 'You might find something in here.' Which I promptly did, in *The Rights of Desire*.

A century after Trijntje's death, in March 1825, the leaders of the only significant attempt at a slave revolt at the Cape were hanged and/or tortured at the same place. Among them was the young man Galant, found guilty of having murdered the two Van der Merwe brothers, Nicolaas and Barend, with whom he had grown up. (At the same time, an in camera trial within the trial brought to light the suggestion of a love affair between Galant and Barend's wife Hester.) The story was first brought to my notice by the historian Hermann Giliomee; and the two thousand-odd pages of testimony from that trial kept in the Cape Archives triggered the writing of *A Chain of Voices*.

These are only two of the slave stories from the Cape that still define the texture of the place. But the memory of them persists, like the shadowy shapes of fish in murky water. Ghosts not yet laid to rest. And it is no surprise to find that Cape Town is indeed a city of ghosts, shades, spectres, revenants. Wherever one goes, there are stories about

---

*An extended version of this early Capetonian horror story is recounted in Mike Nicol's essay, pp 66-76 (Ed).

hauntings. Inevitably in the frowning Castle, less imposing now that it has been dwarfed by surrounding buildings, but still formidable and louring, particularly on a grey day; and also, as can only be expected, in the now rather imposing but once lugubrious Slave Lodge at the top of Adderley Street (where important functionaries of the VOC and stout burghers were allowed visiting hours at night to assuage their pent-up lust, father children on female slaves ranging from the barely nubile to the decrepit, and with Calvinistic righteousness and a sense of patriarchal duty, 'improve the quality of the slave stock in the colony'). The ghosts also frequent the Malay Quarter, which still keeps its dark and dangerous memories behind colourful façades now turned into dollied-up showpieces for the chic and the trendy; Robben Island, where the hazy figure of a drowned nun sometimes shows herself in the mist; the stately home of Kronendal in Hout Bay, to which a beautiful woman forsaken by her beloved returns to rearrange the furniture; the noble old wine estates of Alphen and Constantia; Admiralty House in Simon's Town, still haunted by a 'lady in white', who hanged herself in the 'fisherman's room' two centuries ago; and of course the museum in Simon's Town, where ghosts are almost as much at home as shadows. Among the regular visitors is the benevolent Eleanor in silky black, who invariably leaves behind the scent of lavender; but there are also the more ominous shades of slaves and prisoners in the basement, from a turbulent past with which the present has yet to make its peace.

Through the ghosts one discovers the obvious: that in this place past and present are not opposites, not even terms in juxtaposition. It is, rather, a matter of the past *in* the present, as persistent as a Dalí memory. There are places in Cape Town which in fact exude a sense of timelessness. The museums obviously belong to this dimension. Today there are many more of these than before, the most moving of the additions being those of District Six and Robben Island. The entire experience of the latter, from the moment the ferry leaves the quay to the moment it returns, belongs not so much to time and space as to a state of mind, in which the present and the most recent past – the sojourn of ANC and PAC leaders like Nelson Mandela or Robert Sobukwe – reach back to a more distant history: to the incarceration of great leaders like Makana, and all the way back to the early days of Dutch settlement (an era evoked with such remarkable understanding in Dan Sleigh's monumental novel *Islands*), when the island was a holding space for prisoners, for lepers, for 'undesirable elements'. Among these was that forlorn, exceptional woman Eva (or Krotoa), the first go-between in negotiations involving the Dutch and the Khoi, also the first indigenous woman officially married to a Hollander and one of the first victims of the chain of misunderstanding that defined race relations at the Cape ...

But in my childhood there was, for us, only the museum in the Gardens, where I could spend hours making drawings in a small notebook of all the stuffed mammals; and then stare in awe at the Bushmen in the display cabinets, firmly believing that they, too, had been stuffed and propped up in disconcertingly lifelike postures.

But more timeless, more solid, altogether more majestic than any building, is Table Mountain itself. The exquisite terror that gripped one on a first ascent by cable car. The dassies on the top boulders. The triumphant feeling when a few of us boys could briefly evade the stern surveillance of parents to pee over the edge and watch the thin spray evaporating in the wind. *We are such stuff.* The view from there. The harbour with its ships and cranes and its promise of reaching out to the farthest unknown reaches of the earth. The coastline, an indolent painting in blue and white.

The undulating mountains, past the Twelve Apostles to Cape Point, the petrified monument to the Titan Adamastor, punished for all eternity for his arrogant attempt to seduce the eminently seducible sea-nymph Thetis. And although one knows that Agulhas reaches further south into the ocean than this spindly coccyx of the continent, this *feels* like the end of the earth, the meeting point between two angry oceans, one warm, one cold, where everything is reduced to the elements of earth and air and rock (and sometimes, in summer, fire too), and where there is no obstacle, for thousands of kilometres, between our uncertain here-and-now and the distant icy Antarctic.

But ultimately Cape Town is not an assemblage of places and monuments, of sites and historical spaces: it is an entity defined by its people, a kind of Comtean gathering of all who have gone before, all who are here now, all still to come in the future. The pioneers, the Great Men, the achievers, the illustrious, yes. But also, and especially, the hosts of the ordinary, the humdrum, the mundane: those who, by and large, do not make history but undergo it, as immortalised in Brecht's poem *Fragen eines lesenden Arbeiters* (*Questions from a Worker Who Reads*). The shepherds of fat-tailed sheep, the burghers trying to eke out a living along the Liesbeek; the Khoi victims of colonialist expansion, and the colonial victims of Khoi retaliation; the mothers of many children, the children of dour or generous mothers; those who live in face-brick houses in the northern suburbs, or behind high walls to the south of the mountain; those who survive, or try to survive, in the wind and dust of the Cape Flats and in shacks along the dunes; the street children with big eyes and snotty noses and cupped hands who can curse blue lightning bolts from a clear sky; the bergies pushing their Shoprite or Pick 'n Pay trolleys to gathering points in subways or in parks, smelling of Blue Train and wood-smoke, of mortality and humanity. All of those, countless and nameless, who ensure that the Cape survives. Beautiful and hideous, dangerous and comforting, disconcerting and reassuring. The Cape. The fairest cape in the whole circumference of the earth.

André Brink is Emeritus Professor in the Department of English at the University of Cape Town. His novels have been published in thirty-three languages. Among the awards he has received over the years are the Martin Luther King Memorial Prize (Britain), the Prix Médicis Etranger (France), the Premio Mondello (Italy) and the Monismanien Prize for Human Rights (Sweden). He holds honorary doctorates from universities in Europe and South Africa.

Mark Behr

Cape Town, My Love

The seventeen-year-old blonde boy with the promise of a smile. Initially, that photograph gets me. A small-town kid from the Free State. Here to find a job. A hard-working boy, his father said. The future for him was bright. He called home every morning. First time ever the phone didn't ring his parents knew something was amiss. His body was found among others with names not their own, with years added to his age. How did the police come by this picture? I imagine a mother, fingers wrung numb, tentatively tracing the family-album's page. Which image should she extract for the messengers of state? By this, the world will remember her son.

In the night of 20 January 2003, nine males – seven male-to-male sex workers, a client and the club's owner – were murdered in a Cape Town sex club named Sizzlers. A tenth victim, with his throat slit, two bullets in his head and doused in petrol, loosened the ropes with which he had been bound and escaped. Later, he was able to identify one of the killers from a police photograph relating to a long-forgotten vehicle theft. One black man and one white man were arrested. In court the survivor testified: 'I looked him in the eyes while he slit my throat.'

The accused maintained that a simple robbery had gone awry: they had not planned on killing. Only after one and then another victim resisted did they begin killing. The state countered by asking: if the murders were not premeditated, why had the killers brought with them a knife, hand guns, rope, masking tape, latex gloves, a can of petrol and balaclavas they never bothered to put on? The surviving witness told how the accused had spoken on a cellphone midway through the robbery. The accused invoked their right to silence. The judge pointed out that the murderers had chosen to humiliate their victims before killing them. He expressed dismay at the killers' refusal to speak and make understandable their actions to the victims' loved ones. The accused were found guilty of nine counts of murder and one count of attempted murder. Sentence was life without parole. In his sentence the judge quoted lyrics from a song that could be heard on a video recorded by the police upon arrival at the crime scene: 'Don't be ashamed, let your conscience be your guide. But, oh, know deep inside me, I believe you love me. Forget your foolish pride.'

Questions abounded. Could a crime or drug-syndicate be behind it? Had there been a racial motive? If the objective was robbery, why not target one of the wealthier straight Sea Point sex clubs? Was it significant that one of the killers in an early affidavit had stated that his girlfriend 'had broken my heart with another woman'? Were the murders related to the repeated bombing of city gay bars? And, I wondered: Why didn't they fight back?

The court record suggests that two of the murdered men

did resist. They were the first to be killed. But there had been ten men in the club and only two armed intruders. Ten, surely, could have overpowered two? In court the lone witness said the men in Sizzlers had been 'promised by the killers' that they would not be killed. Jokes had even passed between them. Then they had allowed themselves to be tied up, hands to feet and face down on their stomachs. Did nine men and a seventeen-year-old boy reasonably believe their assailants' 'promise' that they would not be killed? No sign of resistance as they slit their throats. In a city where most people live hand to mouth it is fair to assume any intruder is after money or something to sell. Why risk life or limb in fight or flight? Still, the question kept returning: are some men, often men who have sex with men, so accustomed to placating that even in the face of life-threatening danger they're incapable of confrontation? What, I insisted to my-self, compels anyone to believe a 'promise' from armed men wearing gloves, carrying a can of petrol and not hiding their faces?

But then, perhaps their passivity had nothing to do with a desire to placate. Instead, it had to do with betrayal: sure they'd struck a deal, the sex workers were certain they would not be hurt; but their assailants had lied to them. Deceived was what they were. But, can one be betrayed by people you know already disdain you?

Frowning over the details of a mass murder of gay men in the city (one masseur was said to be straight, had worked merely for the money) and baffled by one so young in the newspaper picture, other times and other voices begin to speak in me. Remembrance of war and youth. Me at eighteen already trained to be a killer. Going to fight on 'the Border'. Of first love in Angola. Pride's proximity to shame. Of me and Joe on a Sea Point balcony. How far, I wondered, were we, at that age in the army, from the boy-man in the

Sea Point brothel?

Nights in Angola, with our watch over and the next sentries on guard, Joe and I lay in our narrow trench on top of a sleeping bag's inner lining. Chest moved against chest. Our feet free of combat boots, heels against soil, toes touching toes, awkwardly and always silently fumbling, vigilant against discovery by our own – even while ours rarely were the only sounds of the night. Once we returned from the war we knew I would go to Cape Town to complete formal officer training in the navy. Joe was assigned to remain at Infantry School in Oudtshoorn. Wordless and barefoot on our last night together in the Charlie Company barracks, we dared not lie down on the dark shower-room cement floor to make our goodbye. Next morning, with a dozen other officer hopefuls, I boarded the train for Simon's Town. Passing mountains and vineyards, rattling through tunnels while laughing with my fellow candidate officers, I cupped my nose to relive the night.

The Cape's beauty exists outside the eyes of the stammering beholder. But on this southern peninsula I found a city and a landscape as captivating as any I could have imagined. For me, it heralded a reprieve from the dust and ochre of our northern war. The Cape spring was liberation from water-less patrols, ammo, webbing, rifle, army rations and the platoon's mortar pipe; Angola forever behind me. But for the separation from Joe, spring here made me feel light, as if life was breaking through for me too: to be eighteen years old and already chosen!

At Mum's request I had a portrait taken that remains framed on Dad's desk: my white shirt ironed flat and clean and hard as blank paper; on the shoulders the black epaulettes with the gold braided insignia; my short thick blonde hair is beginning to turn darker, hinting nothing of the balding to come; my wide open blue eyes confidently hold the camera and at the corners of my mouth, beneath light pink acne scars, a smile waits, held back by something unnamed. The political and ethical significance of soldiering for white South Africa, like the burden of a soldier's guilt and shame, would be a while coming. Then we were fighting communists and terrorists: on the border we kept South Africa safe. At the height of South Africa's war in Angola, forty thousand white boys per year went into the Defence Force. During twenty years of conscription, only enough to count on one hand became conscientious objectors who went to prison. Others – mostly from moneyed backgrounds – left the country. Years passed before I myself became interested in a different grasp of white and black, of rich and poor, of Robben Island, of the beloved city's parasitic cord to the Cape Flats. Not far below my window in the Silvermine Officers' Mess I could see Pollsmoor Prison, where a dissident poet, now incarcerated, once wrote that Cape Town was a 'charming arch-harlot, a slut, a hussy, a tart, a shrew ... not even a mother'. An anarchist, so I believed then, without doubt deserving to be behind bars.

Views described from Table Mountain have beggared a million postcards. Up there you're under earth's widest dome. Below you the City Bowl, whence suburbs, townships and informal settlements fan out along roads and highways of the sandy flats to the Hottentots Holland mountains. Turn your head and before you the continent reaches way down to Cape Point. Oceans glisten to turquoise coves and white beaches. Every season bursts in different flower. Here, you're on top of the world.

Phone calls to Joe on a conscript's salary were out of the question. Instead, swelled by our new status, our ability to inspire awe and even fear, we wrote letters. Of the first salute received and nonchalantly returned; of anticipating the new January intakes. As we never spoke of what we did with or felt for each other, we believed we had little reason to fear the Defence Force censors. 'Colour and water. And beautiful people. Such softness has Cape Town, Joe, after Angola.' Weekly my letters to him conjured the new place. What I could not imagine saying to him, about him or us, I said of the city: 'This place wants to be touched and tasted. Nothing as narrow as a trench or a sleeping bag inner in this city.' We made a date. We'd meet during his first weekend pass. He would collect me from the naval base in his battered VW. We'd spend a weekend in the Sea Point flat of a family friend.

From our Simon's Town classroom you saw clear across False Bay. A particular lesson, presented with the text of *An Officer and a Gentleman* open on our desks, on the etiquette of shore leave in female company: 'You're always on the street-side of the pavement. Your girlfriend is always protected from the traffic. You never let a woman walk on the side of the traffic.' Intoning disdain, our instructor veered to anecdote: Two male naval officers recently had been caught in a car by MPs, in flagrante delicto. They were brought onto full military parade. 'Remember, Midshipmen,' our instructor said, 'this is what happens when an officer gets homo ideas. Base commander or ship's captain marches from the dais to where the disgraced officer waits under the gaze of his entire unit. Ceremonial sword extracted from sheath, the commander uses rapid motions to slice the epaulettes from the disgraced shoulders. Members of the unit do an about-turn so their backs greet the dishonoured. Accompanied by drummers the former officer is drummed from the unit's gates to where he is awaited by civilian police. Here he is arrested and charged with the age-old civil crime of sodomy.'

With those few sentences my anticipation of seeing Joe and of displaying my hard-earned rank instantly turned on me: Unbearable – that word specifically – if anyone ever found out about him and me. I could not have lived with the shame of anyone's knowing that the avowals of rank had been placed upon the shoulders of sedition. Any word from the soldier's dictionary of homophobia spawned fear that one and all of my colleagues would register my discomfort. The only caning I have always remembered in full colour came from a schoolmaster as punishment for a playful sexual romp with other eleven-year-old boys. Sit, we barely could for a week. In the white South African Defence Force, as in the white culture of my youth, only the frequency of racist comments and jokes eclipsed our obsessive repetition of sexist and related faggot/moffie jokes. For a white boy like me, then, nothing ranked lower than being as much as 'suspected' of being homosexual. To ensure we got our performance straight, the culture had us in precision drills, marching, no one out of step, compulsory military cadets from the moment we set foot in high school. The merging of militarisation, sexuality, self-denial and the maintenance of male privilege (white, in our case and era) had been well internalised by the time we woke in shame from our first wet dreams. Self-loathing and vigilance against ourselves did not start during our years in the army's pay, but it was often fine-tuned during that masquerade: strip them of rank and send them to jail for playing with one another's willies; bedeck their flat chests with medals for killing.

I wrote to Joe that I would be unable to rendezvous at the gates of SAS *Simon's Town*. In a response that picked carefully at words but barely concealed its plea, he convinced me to meet him at the Sea Point flat. I recognised the VW parked at the roadside along the green that separates Sea Point from the ocean. I stepped from the elevator into the lyrics of Freddie Mercury's 'Bohemian Rhapsody'. Joe had set out a bottle of Tassenberg and two glasses on the balcony. In the setting sun, with the wine ignored, I strained to tell him that I was not staying. Men needn't be soldiers to deceive themselves and others the way I did when I said: 'The thing that happened between us was once off. You know, men in prison and men in the army. Men isolated or hard up will fuck a donkey.' His dark eyes brimmed. What I would not, could not even contemplate saying was: 'I would rather die than have anyone find out about us. And so, I terminate this love in remittance for respectability.'

As if sharing my thoughts – himself having long ago decoded me-him-us and what was required of our kind to survive in this world we so proudly occupied – he suggested that no one need ever know: we could finish National Service, go to university, get married and have children and still 'do this without anyone ever knowing'. For an instant I was ready to embrace his vision. Was this not the way everyone did it? I imagined us together forever: never having to pay the price of revelation. While the cost for wives and children never crossed my mind, I shook my head. Again I insisted that what 'had happened' had meant nothing important, that we had to move on.

He cleared his throat as I started to leave. He was looking out to Robben Island. I would remember only his profile as he smiled, saying: 'Nothing as narrow as a trench or a sleeping bag here in Cape Town, eh, Mark?' That took me only months rather than years to grasp.

On the street I wondered whether he was still up on the balcony. Looking down on me. Nearing his parked car, I recognised the registration letters of the small town where his parents lived. Their congregation had set up a fund to send Joe to university where he would study to become a dominee in the Dutch Reformed Church. I walked away, absurdly repeating the car's registration number for blocks, not allowing myself a glance back.

I have heard soldiers speak of killing less from fear of being killed themselves than from the shame of being known as a man unable to kill: as if the capacity for killing and for brutality is presupposed only in the signifier 'man' alone. When men speak thus, one may understand killing or aggression as performed most profoundly from a shame related to awareness that none of us is quite 'the man' we are supposed or meant to be. Not being tough in the army translated into being unable to have a woman (on your inside of the pavement), which collapsed further into being queer – the latter akin to but somehow lower or more dangerous than being a woman. To not be woman or woman-like. To not betray maleness and your sex by showing yourself falling short – even as the neurotic jokes showed straight depending for its lifeblood on queer. By acting tough, we hoped against hope, believed that pretending together with privilege would ensure the promised protection.

A decade later, after other towns, teachers, countries and other texts had helped remake me, I went to live in Vredehoek on the slopes of Table Mountain. On a switchbacking path not dissimilar to the one stomped open by tens of millions of lesbians, homos, queens and transvestites the world over, I stepped out in Cape Town's newly established Gay Pride Parade. Within months South Africans voted in their first democratic election. Through lobbying, activism and moral imagination political elites were moved to overcome blind spots on sexual and gender discrimination. South Africa famously became the first country in the world to include sexual orientation with other key protections in its new constitution: some time soon, men would even be able to marry men. Inconceivable! People of alternative sexualities and genders now had a legal foothold from which to extend their struggles against heterosexism and bigotry. New ways of engaging personal and political power were being realised.

White Cape Town was drawn closer to the people who did most of the city's work. Treasuries that had for three and a half centuries safeguarded, nursed, fed, transported and educated only a few, were opened to begin acknowledging citizens who lived mostly beyond the city's older streets.

In those days I went to visit a friend whose home was a haven for sick gay men. I recognised Joe at once. We gave each other big hugs and he held me in his skinny and generous arms. Neither of us spoke of Sea Point. Neither of us had come out yet to our parents; I was preparing to; he doubted he would: not because of their disappointment at him having not become a *dominee*, but as their self-righteousness about everything from sex to the rising crime rate to Nelson Mandela's presidency had snuffed out any care he'd once had for them. I did not say: but our actions also once upheld that man's incarceration. Instead, I asked about Joe's health: surely he would tell his parents that he was ill? Let them find out after I'm dead, he shrugged. We spoke of Namibia gaining independence and Angola haltingly coming into itself. An estimated ten million mines remained planted there that someone would have to track and defuse. A decade after we had left Angola, around one hundred and twenty people per month continued to be maimed or killed by landmines – some of which we had planted. We shook our heads in disbelief, denial or self-delusion and spoke of other things.

Despite his loss of weight and the years, I found Joe beautiful. Had gauntness and age enhanced his looks, or had I in that interregnum learnt to acknowledge the beauty of men? The prospect of successful antiretroviral treatment was still a few years off, and I couldn't but wonder how long he could live. When I returned from an annual teaching obligation in Europe, he was gone. I wondered whether I should contact his parents. If I did, what would I say to them? Your son and I knew each other for less than a year as eighteen-year-old soldiers a decade ago. We briefly were lovers. We were both closeted, but he was in a sense braver than I. We saw each other recently – once only – after a night that took place years ago on a balcony in Sea Point. He had AIDS and he was beautiful and very angry with you and with himself. Had I been as brave as he, perhaps I too would be ill. Could I say this to his family? Surely I could offer very little with integrity that they would wish to hear. None of my current friends knew Joe nor had anyone known how important he had been in my life. Like his parents, I would mourn him on my own, in my own way write my own elegy to him, to us, our time.

The mountain is a foggy blue-grey in the morning when I head through the old Company Gardens for the High Court archives, the only place to access the full transcript of the Sizzlers trial. The file is thicker than my forearm on the desk. What I had not anticipated are the photographs from the scene of the crime. I will have to see men tied up with their throats slit. I will have to see that blonde boy slaughtered. Do I want these images in my head? My motives for indeed turning the page I do not quite understand. But, when I do, I keep my focus to one side.

Against a wall is a set of cheap bunk beds where they slept when they were not working. A book lies open. A novel maybe, whose title I cannot make out. There are clothes that have been dropped to wear again tomorrow. I allow my gaze the slightest inward shift. In some pictures the bodies are almost neatly in a row. A few are on their sides, some with their chests to the carpet, ankles tied behind their backs to their wrists. Like quails prepared for the roast. They are dressed in jeans. Some shirts are unbuttoned. Every body looks like that of a teenaged boy, yet most of them were in their twenties. Here is a sparse trail of hair up to a navel. I strain to keep my eyes off their faces. It is the youthfulness of the bodies, the taut skin that strikes me, over and over. The blonde boy could be any one of these bodies. How terribly thin are these arms! How defenceless these fingertips! This man, this boy too, somehow wrestled himself onto his side. The vulnerability of their hands and their feet tied back is overwhelming. Still I keep my eyes from venturing to their faces and necks. Who is boy and who is man I cannot say. Which one are you? Not the blood on the ceiling or the brutalisation of the twisted bodies and limbs, nothing of what is gruesome catches me. Not the empty cartridges flung onto the carpet. Instead, it is how utterly and despairingly frail these men look. For an instant, images of other bodies disremembered drift into memory. But here, now, the carpet beneath the blood-painted white bodies is red, patterned with squares of white and grey. Now my eyes go further back over the frayed carpet: someone must have used that bottle of tomato sauce for dinner; there is a small box of Smarties open; a crumpled Liquifruit container, apricot flavour, with its straw still protruding. Was this what you were drinking when they came in? I imagine your fear. Your panic. My eyes catch sight of a flip-flop still held between the toes of one skinny upturned foot.

Unbearable.

I leave the basement archives and climb back to street level. With the notepad still in hand I walk back into the Gardens. Here slaves mostly from the East once cultivated fruit and vegetables for the Dutch East India Company. On Government Avenue the statue of Cecil John Rhodes still has an arm raised to the north above the inscription: 'Your hinterland is there.' There is the Tuynhuys, city home to successive prime ministers and presidents. Is it too soon to guess at ironic inscriptions beneath future statues to President Thabo Mbeki, the current occupant of that house?

The oaks, leafless now, colossal trunks disappearing beneath the earth, were brought in from Europe centuries ago. The Camellia japonicas are in full, dust-red bloom. Black and white children in the same primary-school uniforms dash after a squirrel, crash through a patch of seeding clivias and disappear trailing laughter. And then I remember the black bodies.

Between the South African Museum and the National Gallery I find a bench in the sun. The sky is bright now; the mountain a grey mammoth against blue. I write: The last images I have of Cape Town boys spread out in death – not on carpeting, but on tarmac and dust – are from a Truth and Reconciliation Commission hearing not far from here. The images were shown during an amnesty application by one white and one black policeman for their parts in the murder of the Guguletu Seven. Mothers of the seven murdered boys came to hear what had been done to their sons. Astonished in grief, these women watched a video of their children's bodies and then faced their children's killers. Arbitrarily chosen black boys – sons of migrant men and women in search of work in the city – had been framed by the state. Picked up off the street they were told they were being trained for the struggle. Instead, at a moment when the minority government required anti-terrorist propaganda to justify its 'total strategy', the boys were gunned down – by the very people that had trained them. I recall video footage of young bodies angled for maximum effect. Feet-first to the cameras. Their feet are made to look too big. Weapons have been conspicuously placed near their brown fingertips. Ropes are used dramatically to turn over and drag lifeless young bodies for the camera and the world to better see. Their faces, all shades of brown, are somehow all erased.

The murders were carried out in the late Eighties. Was it '86, or '87? The time when white conscripts like Joe and me and the rest of Charlie Company were withdrawn from Angola to be deployed in this city's townships. 'Where is the border now?' demanded graffiti from the underpass on Buitenkant Street.

We could have been there, Joe, you and I. We were so good with guns. But, could we have fought back? Could our soldiering have spelt salvation or merely more deception? Would shame, an impulse to appease, a knife or our terror of drummers on parade have united us again to allow ourselves to be tied up? From those trenches, could I have found a voice to say: I looked my killer in the eyes while he slit my throat. Back then I'd rather kill than have anyone find out about us. My love, were feet ever as vulnerable as when we were officers and gentlemen, trained as killers and so very proud of it?

Mark Behr was born in Tanzania in 1963. He was educated in South Africa, Norway and the United States. He is the author of two novels, The Smell of Apples and Embrace. His work has been translated into eight languages and has received awards in Africa, the United Kingdom and the United States of America. He travels annually between South Africa and Santa Fé, New Mexico, where he is an Associate Professor of World Literature and Fiction Writing.

Marlene van Niekerk

To Behold the Cape

The game went as follows. My father would stand behind me and pull my ears upwards.

Can you see the Cape? He would ask.

The fingers shifted their grip, tugged at your ears with ever more conviction. At last you had to concede, protesting, laughing, wriggling. And to escape, you had to see it, large as life, true as true, Cape Town, dazzling and clear with mountain and sea and skyscrapers.

Do you remember the game, I ask my father on my last visit to Kleinmond. He does not hesitate, laughs, of course he remembers, nowadays he forgets so much, but that he remembers.

Do you see the Cape.

He brings his hands to his ears. His eyes look, unseeing, into the distance.

Good thing he can still find his ears, my mother's glance signals to me.

She fetches the photo albums from the hall cupboard. I fetch my reading glasses. I page through the first family album with my mother and father. Caledon 1948 to 1959, it says on the cover. The album has brown pages and the photos were taken with a box camera, sometimes out of focus, the figures floating as in a seance.

My father peers and frowns under the lamp over the dining table, he can no longer read the captions written under each photo in my mother's emphatic hand.

Clean your glasses, says my mother to my father.

Where are the days, says my father.

We drove to Cape Town from Caledon in a Vauxhall with a maroon roof and a light cream body.

Six hundred and seventy-six pounds it cost, straight from the box, says my father, and presses his finger on the photo, can you believe it, six cylinders, I always took off the rims to clean them properly. You remember, you couldn't say Vauxhall, says my father, his gaze shifting between now and then, Bawkdawl you said, your mouth round as an O.

You can remember very well when you want to, my mother says askance to my father.

The album pages are rigid, the photos are mounted with old-fashioned black corners. I remember the white box in which the corners were kept, a welter of corners if you emptied them on the green formica top of the kitchen table of my childhood, magic black corners, so that once cornered and pasted, each photo was charmed into a fairy tale in front of your eyes. Young man with new car, young woman with first child, small child with first nursery rhyme book and glasses. I remember the pasting sessions, the smell of the inside of the sideboard where the albums were kept, the proliferation of albums in those dark recesses, the bulky actuality of history. I try to remember, tap at my father's and mother's memories.

I was on my mother's lap the first time we went to Cape Town, and the trip, from then on every six months for all of three years, was singly for my sake.

Because I was born with Ouma Lenie's lazy eye.

Inherited, says my mother, I was ever so unhappy, you with your curly locks like Shirley Temple.

Whatever happened to Shirley Temple? I ask.

Actress, you know, says my mother, the usual route. She makes a gesture of irrevocable decline.

Eye science was in Cape Town. They selected the best ophthalmologist in town for me. His name was Ferreira. Jan Ferreira.

I made you count the colours on the way to Cape Town, that first time we went, says my father, it was September, *Vat jou goed en trek, Ferreira,** I sang for you so that you shouldn't be scared and I taught you about green. The green of barley, the green of corn, the green of lucerne, blue-green of a plot of onions, the yellow of wild mustard, yellow of sorrel, purple of heather at Bot River, until you could tell them all apart. And we counted, you and I, three white lambs against the dam wall, six little pink pigs in the bean patch. Nothing wrong with your vision, I told your mother, says my father, quick of mind is quick of eye.

You with your proverbs, says my mother to my father.

Bawkdawl, I say, had a gear, here, right next to the steering wheel, a gear lever with a kink in it, and a handle on the end.

Right, says my father, you remember well, it was before the days of stick shifts.

I see in my mind's eye my father's hand, a slender and smooth hand without age spots, resting on the lever, changing gears, jauntily with an open palm, for the ascent

---

*Afrikaans folk song. Get your stuff and move on, Ferreira.

in a wide circle over the known earth.

Did somebody say then: Look back, look through the back window, that's what heaven looks like?

And who called 'Houw Hoek!' in the wet grey-green heart of the Hottentots Holland Mountains?

And then, hold your breaths – who sees, who sees, who sees the sea first? And at last the opening up of the view, the descent over the wide bay of the new world. False Bay. And its light blue nourisher and guardian, Table Mountain. The other side of heaven.

De zon en de zee springen bliksemend open, wij gaan naar het paradijs. (Sun and sea leap open in lightning, we are leaving for paradise.) Did these lines of Marsman make such a deep impression on me later on because of those first childhood descents from Sir Lowry's Pass over the bay, the weltering waters traced with silver sparkling? Of the browns, the greens, of the Overberg this was the contrary. It was blue, all blue, blue was the colour of the Cape.

And then there was the second great symphonic view, just as you crest the rise of De Waal Drive, the harbour, the ships, the cranes with bent heads, the bandy legs of the breakwaters arcing out beyond the harbour mouth.

Next a fountain blowing an arc out of a round dam I remember, and my father's voice: Look there, Karlientjie. Jan van Riebeeck in his plus-fours, with his walking stick planted at a jaunty angle and hat with the ostrich feather, the first white man under Table Mountain. Plume of water, plume of bronze.

Jan Pierewiet, I said.

Van Riebeeck, my father corrected.

*Jan Pierewiet, Jan Pierewiet, Jan Pierewiet staan stil,** I sang.

---

*Afrikaans folk song. Jan Pierewiet, stand still.

My father and mother look at each other over the album, they can't remember the name of the building to which we used to go. Near the top end of Adderley Street. The Medical Centre?

The consulting room was a large twilit space, red lights and green lights and a bare illuminated screen glowing against the far wall, all sorts of instruments, control panels.

Ferreira was in the shadows, his large black moustache I could make out, quick of laughter, a white coat, a little lamp in front of his head, a stentorian voice.

Up and in you go, Karlientjie, said my father and lifted me into the monstrosity.

That was the worst, I say, a flapped-open tomb of black leather, a high back, a broad seat, a chair for blind giants, the seat of the one-eyed king of the underworld.

If you say so, my child, says my father with a chuckle.

The doctor placed large cool hands on my face, there were coarse black hairs on his fingers.

Look, he said, look at doctor, at the tip of his nose.

Tip of Ferreira's nose. *Vat jou goed en trek, Ferreira.* In the background was my father wiping his face a few times, and my mother, her face concerned, her gaze sharpened.

Hmm, said the doctor, hmmm, and is daddy going to buy you an ice cream when we've done?

He moved his finger slowly to and fro in front of me.

Hmm, he said, let's look at pictures. Do you like pictures?

A tall contraption on a stilt, an angel on castors, a monster with a stove-in head the doctor rolled into position behind my chair. Then he folded out two black wings and swung them in front of my face.

You are here, my father said to me, and mommy and daddy are here, we're staying right here, touch your nose.

Beat your arms past the wings, fly past the flight of the

146

black angel, find your face between his wings, you are there, you touch a nose, it's yours. The time granted you, the sight and the insight, the inkling and the dream. The beginning of it all, the origin of all tales.

And then eyeholes open in the stark shut walls and the eyelids of an angel begin to blink in your stead, click, click, click, little rings of lenses that fall apart in a cascade of tiny portholes. The prospect of divergent perspectives opens up and of enlarged miniatures, the worlds of the binoculars, the magnifying glass, the microscope, the camera lens. The drama of the fall of the shutter permanently grooved in your inner eye.

Shame, you were really quite anxious, I came and sang to you, do you remember, my father asks.

As Jan vir Karlientjie doodslaan, o wee o wee, my father sings on the rainy day in April in Kleinmond, *oor die see oor die see met die oorlogsteamer mee.**

Hottentot songs, says my mother.

Aye, the days, says my father and looks at me.

I remember Ferreira's pictures for the eye test. The rainbow, the fishes, the animals, the moon and the sun and the firmament full of stars. A man, a woman, a hand, a tree, a dragon with fire-breathing nostrils, an apple, and the ark of Noah. Not a bit difficult, I knew all the names of what God created on earth and was good, and I did not doubt their outlines.

And then came the statue on a pedestal.

Jan Pierewiet! I shouted, it's Jan Pierewiet!

The doctor laughed, my mother and father laughed.

Jan van Riebeeck it was.

Ferreira put the arms of the black angel into my hands,

---

*Afrikaans folk song. If Jan kills Karlientjie, oh my oh my, across the sea, across the sea, on board the wartime steamship.

two cold black gear levers.

Well then, come, he said, let's see if you can put Jan Pierewiet back on his pedestal, I could swear he's fallen off.

And indeed, through one peephole I could see the pedestal and through the other the plus-fours with his hat plume and his walking stick groping its way in emptiness.

Just like Humpty Dumpty. Had a great fall.

I tried like all the king's horses and all the king's men but I couldn't get Jan back on his pedestal.

And then we had to hear that your eyes don't coordinate, says my mother, the one eye is far-sighted and the other one near-sighted, and the one eye sees well but the other sees only twenty-five percent, and you need glasses and you have to go around with cotton wool over the strong eye so that the weak one can be exercised. Oh dear oh dear oh dear me.

Dis te ver om te loop, dis te na om te ry, my father hums. He interrupts his tune. And then, your mother wanted tea with lots of sugar in the Koffiehuis next to the Groote Kerk and when we walked in there was a gathering of black toecaps with solemn snouts sip-sipping at thick-lipped cups and I said not a whit surrounded by this lot of holy toads, let's go and eat peanuts with the squirrels in the Gardens and ice cream from a cart and then we go to the Parade and buy samoosas and bananas, a double bunch, a bunch from Canaan, with ten bananas this side and ten on the other.

And as we left, walking out of the super-sanctified Afrikaner Koffiehuis, says my father, I bought your mother daffodils from a friendly Muslim woman, a bunch like that, and your mother still wanted to stop me, no Jack this and no Jack that, yes I was still Jack then, we don't have any water, they'll just wilt, and I said to her they're welcome to

*Afrikaans folk song. It's too far to walk, it is too near to ride.

148

wilt, love never wilts, I married her and she's my wife and we'll stand by each other through thick and thin, far-sighted, near-sighted, coordination or not, and to me she looks so pretty with a daffodil, I told your mother, and her hair was still black in those days, my Marie with the raven hair on a spring day in Cape Town.

My father winks at me.

Lawks, but what a stream of nonsense you can talk, my mother says.

My father checks up on the rain outside. I remember that day in Cape Town, he says, your mother was on the brink of tears. So I thought, if the daffodils don't do the trick perhaps the pulpit will, so I went and showed you the pulpit in the Groote Kerk, do you remember, mother?

My mother gives my father a l-o-o-o-ng look.

And then, after the pulpit and after the Gardens and after the Parade, and every time we were in Cape Town for your eyes, we just had to go to Garlicks once more and so I trawled along, says my father, because there was nothing like curtaining or a dress pattern to lift your mother's spirits. Garlicks, that I do remember, all roads lead to Garlicks, where frail old English ladies with hats and gloves and rouge on their cheeks sit and eat scones with red jam and cream. And Mother leafing, with spurious attention, with unappeasable longing, through hefty pattern books, their names like goddesses, like djinns of eternally slimmed long-necked femininity, McCalls, Vogue, Simplicity, and thump thump on the counter the cloth is rolled down and the sales lady, so recently all whispering gentleness, changes suddenly into a fury and tears, after a short incision, the floral cloth with a single fell stroke, garrrr! down the middle, her gold tooth flashing like a bolt of lightning.

And then the return was upon us. Back over the mountain, back over the hills and the dales, with all the treasures of the Cape, with its far blue views. At home in a bowl the bananas flavoured the kitchen for a week, and a rustling dress pattern was pinned to the new cloth in the sitting room on the red carpet. My first pair of glasses arrived by post, and the thick wad of cotton wool folded in gauze was placed under one lens to shade out my strong eye so that it looked as if I'd been in an accident. It scratched and misted up and itched. With the lazy eye I was the denizen of a hazy world and unsure of my coming and my going.

I remember the half-yearly exercises with Miss Thompson, the ophthalmologist's understudy, the lion I could not get to go into its cage, the train not back onto the tracks, Shirley Temple not on the straight and narrow. For three years the tests and the therapy continued and Dr Ferreira's pictures got more and more complicated as I got older. A ball on top of a man on top of a horse in a circus tent. A child in a cradle in a room. A man and a woman in a hall in a mirror.

Looking back, Cape Town was for me the origin of a visual disarticulation of the everyday, the eye test a kind of training in double sense. A fortunate misfortune. An irreversible realisation of the process of vision took place in those black chairs, the eye ever after a suspicious Geiger counter along everyday surfaces, an amperometer of plaster, bark and meniscus. Surfaces mere membranes over precipices, distances reeled in to close-by, the whole sea in the jaw of a fish, paradise in a sparaxis flower, an angel in a stone. All my life I shall continue to gaze at the moon through binoculars, magnificent silver thrush of the night.

A kind of foreshortening of the imagination I contracted in the Cape of eye tests. Henceforth I could perversely prune back reality, distil the widest panorama to some essence. It made of me a snow globe fetishist for life. You could turn everything round, make everything bigger or smaller, and trace connections between an umbrella and a foot, a squirrel and a coffee pot. The Cape as cradle of metaphor, dry dock of metonymy. Table Mountain a sublime miniature, my eyes the storerooms of disjunct detail which I tumbled to and fro over the over of the Overberg as in a private kaleidoscope. I transferred the Cape therapies to the hills of my childhood, the contours of harvested cornfields telescoped to the fine lines of the fingerprint of a very large giant. A great blue giant of the Riviersonderend mountains, he who leaves the imprint of his sparkling palms on the round hills, the blessing of Klipdale, the baptism of the foreheads of the silos of Protem.

The later albums confirm the obsessive gaze. On these photos, now without corners, all of them slid in behind transparent plastic layers on the sticky album page, there is the record of a family holiday in the late Sixties. Me with a magnifying glass next to a silver tree in Kirstenbosch, next to a scrawl on the wall of the slave pit in the Castle. On top of Table Mountain I peer through a telescope at the ships in the bay. At Cape Point bedraggled in a red pinafore with a black strap around my neck.

Do you remember, that was after a baboon got hold of your camera through the car window, says my mother – you let off the flash in his face.

Where are the days, says my father. And that was the Cape when you were small. When the world was young. And now you have been to so many places all over the world.

Yes, says my mother, born with a golden spoon in her mouth. She shows a photo of me peeping through a hole in my fist at two swans on the frozen North Sea at Hoorn, 1985. I can't remember who photographed me there, but I do remember that I selected the photo from a whole range to send to them.

I have to get going, I say.

Which road will you take. Along the sea or Sir Lowry's?

What do you think then, I ask my father.
Watch where you go, says my father, on the old routes.
He laughs with me. He knows what I'm thinking of.
Do you see the Cape.

Marlene van Niekerk was born near Caledon in 1954. She attended school in Riviersonderend and Stellenbosch, and then the University of Stellenbosch. In 1979 she moved to Germany to join theatres in Stuttgart and Mainz. She is now Professor in the Department of Afrikaans and Dutch at Stellenbosch University. Her books include two volumes of poetry, a collection of short stories, and the acclaimed novels *Triomf* and *Agaat*.

Luke West

Room with Open Window

At ten thousand metres above sea level something happens to my ankles. They swell up, and press hard against the ridges of my shoes. Even when the captain switches the cabin lights off and the dinner trays have been cleared, I can't sleep. I toss and turn, sigh, get a drink of water, stuff toilet paper in my ears.

The plane makes a gentle hum as we move down the West Coast. On a video screen in front of me the flight path is shown in simple blues and reds, while the speed and distance are displayed to the right of the map.

As we fly, I glance at the photograph of you sitting in my lap. You lean against a car parked on Signal Hill. Your arms are crossed and you smirk, almost as if you did not want the picture to be taken. Your hair, pulled loosely back in a ponytail, sets the smooth, almost child-like angle of your jaw in relief.

Behind you, Table Mountain is a blue wave peaking be-

153

fore breaking. I can see Tafelberg Road running from the cableway to the bottom of Devil's Peak and, below that, reaching up to the road, the white homes of the City Bowl, like fingers splayed from the centre of the city's hand.

One hour before I land, the plane breaks through the meniscus of clouds and the Cape Peninsula unrolls itself. I have seen it more than two dozen times but the effect is always the same: my heart speeds up; my hands grow clammy; my forehead, when I press it firm against the window, chills.

Over the loudspeaker, the captain announces our descent, and the plane shudders down a few thousand feet. Children scream from the pressure in their ears; the seatbelt light blinks on.

And then we are out, the sky releasing us, the shacks of Khayelitsha burning in the morning sunlight. Peering through the foggy window, I see luminescent figures on the runway marshalling vehicles. One of the drivers waves to the captain as we taxi into our landing bay. I brush my hands through my hair and, taking a deep breath, prepare to meet you.

Your hair has bleached a translucent blonde in the past few months, the result of sun and surf. The rest of your appearance is as I remembered. Your eyes – which, unlike stars, do not dull when you look directly at them – are the same deep amber-green. Your back is perfectly erect as you drive.

How was your flight? you ask.

Okay.

Did you sleep?

I never sleep on planes. You know that.

I thought this time you had pills.

They didn't work, I sigh. The air coming under the Beetle's hood is hot. I roll down the window. High, sandy embankments border the highway. For a time it feels as if we are below sea level, looking up at thousands of shacks. To the right, against the blackened water treatment towers, shacks of plastic rustle in the wind.

As we drive, I try to feel within myself a sense of homecoming. Those dark smudges of trees against Table Mountain. The viscous Liesbeek beside the road. The beat-up cars clattering beside us. The sky hanging over us like a frayed blue blanket. Is this where I want to spend the rest of my life? Have I come home?

We join the M3 heading toward Muizenberg. The air grows cooler as Newlands Forest washes over us. I remember, for a split second, days as a child spent mushrooming, scanning fallen logs and rushing wildly to collect more than my friends. Then the road curves right, up past the opulence of Bishopscourt to Wynberg Hill, offering a clear view of False Bay.

It's good to see you.

It's good to see you, too, I say.

The car rattles down the cobblestones of Anderson Road towards the Kalk Bay harbour. From here the village and the ramparts of the harbour jutting out into the ocean almost look medieval, marred by the occasional palm tree, whose branches, like the sparks of a firework, form a continuous explosion above us.

After parking the car, we are shuffled through the front door of my parents' house. It is a large, castle-like structure built in the Fifties, with a neat garden in front and a balcony overlooking the ocean. My mother is dressed in a blue blouse and wears a pair of small, academic eyeglasses. My grandmother smells of lavender perfume.

My boy, my mother says, hugging me.

Tea arrives on a gold tray with a side plate of fruit cake

and my grandmother's special cookies. We quickly get down to the business of questions: What is New York like? Have I met any famous writers? What about the restaurants? And my apartment? Am I getting along with my housemate? Does it take a long time to get from Brooklyn to the university?

Strangely, although I am happy to see them, throughout the ensuing conversation with my family I find it hard to focus. I find myself fiddling with the teacup and saucer. I eat more of the cookies than I should to give my hands something to do. I keep talking, but I concentrate less on what I say than the way the light, outside, bleaches the white balcony table. Beyond, I see ships moving fluidly in the bay, birds shivering on telephone wires, a palm branch rising and falling.

Perhaps a part of me is still in the plane, I think, circling, waiting for the wheels to touch ground. Is this why the city still has a hazy aura to it, as if shielded from my eyes? Is this why my whole body feels numb?

I happen at this time to be reading Milan Kundera's *The Unbearable Lightness of Being*. It is my third attempt at this difficult novel, and during the family siesta after tea, in which my stepfather watches cricket and you go for a jog, I page back and forth between the covers and feel, finally, that I am getting it. By the word 'light' Kundera wants us to understand meaninglessness, a state of being with no fixed constant with which to orientate itself. The lightness of being allows us to travel anywhere, metaphorically speaking, unburdened by the past which would fix meaning. Yet, as the title of the novel suggests, this state of being is unbearable; we are exiles without a home.

Or not quite. In the final scene, the lovers Tomas and Tereza, having removed themselves from the city to live on a collective farm, mount the stairs to their bedroom. Kundera writes:

Tomas turned the key and switched on the ceiling light. Tereza saw two beds pushed together, one of them flanked by a bedside table and lamp. Up out of the lampshade, startled by the overhead light, flew a large nocturnal butterfly that began circling the room.

Kundera intends the circling of the moth to signify our desire for eternal return, in this case the eternal need for a meaningful human relationship, two beds pushed together to make one. That the moth desires to return eternally to the light – meaninglessness – is significant, since this closing image captures perfectly the existential paradox the novel is at pains to illustrate: that we will not feel at home until we have acknowledged our own essential homelessness, but that this acknowledgement is unbearable.

As the afternoon progresses, I compare my experience of homecoming to my imagined ideal of homecoming. Have I returned to a city that gives me 'weight'? And what would that feel like? If I have come home, I think, then returning to Cape Town should set the rest of my life into a perspective that grants it meaning; it should fix any wandering into the context of having a spiritual home. Is this how I feel? Is the city, for me, really a 'weight'?

Returning from your jog, sweating and with your hair slicked back, you find me again sitting on the balcony, spacing out to a view of the ocean and the mountains across the bay.

Whatcha thinking about? you ask, coming up beside me.

I'm thinking of home, I reply. Whether I've come home. What that means.

And?

I close my eyes. The imprint of the sunlight dancing on the waves is branded on the inside of my eyelids: for a second or two it is as if my eyes are still open, that the ocean, the bay, they are all there, darkened only vaguely, as a photograph grows grainy with time.

I think I've come home, I say slowly, but that coming home is not what I expected.

Yes, but you've come home to me, you reply.

That's true. I have come home to you.

Kundera would say that is impossible, I think quietly to myself. The moth circles endlessly, believing the light is its home, but the moth is misguided – home is only a place in which we feel elsewhere.

Do you sense this distance within me? When we take an early evening stroll down to Main Road, the light buttery on the antique stores and the new restaurants, do you know that I'm not present, that everything, from the view of the sea, to the light, to the mountains, brings me into a space where I imagine foreign spices on an eager tongue, espressos in a Parisian café, a vision of myself in a new suit, smiling, handing out autographs or roses or books? Do you feel the same? Is it Cape Town that does this to us? And why?

After dinner, we climb into the bed in the guest bedroom. We will be staying here for the next week and a half until I fly back to New York. The light in the room is dusty. Cardboard boxes, stacked high against the walls, hold forgotten teacups, bowls, and some of my grandfather's books from the war. If I peel back the curtain, across the vegetable garden and the knife-edge of our neighbour's roof I can make out a buttress of the Kalk Bay mountains.

I let the curtain fall, guillotining the light. You are breathing deeply beside me, exhausted from the tension and excitement of seeing me again after so many months. In that time, I was present only through email and phone. What photographs I saw of you felt like photographs from which my own figure had been cut.

A sudden shudder passes through me. I think inadvertently of Kundera's Tomas, sleeping with whomever he comes across; and then I think of his partner Tereza sniffing these other women on his fingers. As often happens to me in the dark, my heart begins to pound. It feels like there is a man beating on the inside of my ribcage, trying to get out. It seems the earlier thoughts about home, and the impossibility of home, have left me suspicious. Have you been faithful?

You slide closer.

Everything okay?

Yes. Shh.

You seem tense.

I'm not tense.

The floorboards creak as my stepfather returns from the bathroom.

Okay. You yawn. You want to talk?

Not really.

You sure?

Positive. Let's get some sleep.

The following morning Cape Town is again crystalline, the wind up, the smog washed away. On the surface of the sea whitecaps flirt gaily. Breakfast is toast, grapefruit and coffee, served on the balcony. Life is a renewed pleasure.

We decide to go for a hike, parking the car a kilometre or two back along Boyes Drive. The trail, once it has risen halfway up the ridge, cuts horizontally through yellow-wood forests and bluffs sparked with silver trees into long fingers of cool shade. I try for a good hour to press down my suspicions, but to no avail.

Sweetheart, I say.

Yes?

Can I ask you something?

Of course.

I take a deep breath. I had a dream last night. It wasn't the first time. And in the dream.

Yes?

In the dream you –

I'm listening, you say.

Without warning my heart speeds up. I hold my head high to get my bearings. There is the half-moon of False Bay with the hard, flat ovals of surfers out at sea. There is the road below us, and St James pool, and the homes huddled against the slope.

I halt and, blinking my eyes rapidly, take a long sip of water.

Are you okay?

Fine. I brush your concern aside with the cap of the water bottle. I feel fine. Never mind about the dream. I don't know what I was talking about.

Okay. There's a yacht out there, you point. Rounding the corner.

We watch the yacht rounding the corner. The sails are full. It slices fast through the water, leaving the stitches of white scars in its wake.

Are you sure you're okay?

No.

What's wrong?

I don't know.

You slide your arms around my waist.

Let's go, I say. Let's just forget about it.

We push up past a small bowl in the mountains called the Amphitheatre and onto the moonscape on the top of the ridge. Gnarled boulders cast shadows with many heads, and the grass is low to the ground. A small rodent of some kind with brown fur pokes its head out of a hole in the ground to stare at us, then scurries away.

Soon we have more or less lost our way. The guidebook we are using does not help – we are warned that the way gets hard to follow, and that we must watch for beacons. But we cannot find any.

When the truth finally comes, we are sitting at a picnic table at the Kalk Bay Harbour and the salt cellar has just burst over my side-serving of fries. You speak tearfully, flushed with shame, as if the person who did this is someone you no longer know but who has nevertheless called you up out of the blue and taken residence on your couch. Why won't she just go away? You never meant this to happen. You do not know what you were thinking.

I spike my fries one by one with the plastic fork and tap them on the counter to remove the salt.

Oh, I say.

And we all have moments of weakness –

Yes.

And you were far away –

That's true.

And the important thing now is that we are together, and this won't ever, ever happen again.

In the days that follow, I turn to what I can still trust, the landscape of this peninsula, which reflects back to me what has grown opaque in your eyes: a future in which I am happy, secure, and content. I spend days on end hiking, leaving early in the morning and coming home past dark.

My experience of Cape Town has always been one of looking down. Whether this is while driving along Boyes Drive and searching for the surfers below, or during a pause up the steep Kasteelspoort hike, or, like today, when I have simply taken fifteen minutes to escape, like Icarus, and established both a literal and a metaphorical distance between myself and the earth below, I am always rising.

Beyond the granite pillars of Rhodes Memorial, I can see the small, dark shapes of children playing in a field at my old school, St Joseph's. The highways roaring north to Johannesburg, and east to Port Elizabeth and East London, remind me of veins of silver.

The transformative charm of the pastoral has always been what I admire most about the work of Ernest Hemingway. Continually in his novels we find the juxtaposition of anti-heroes trying to escape themselves against the immutable, and somehow transcendent, force of the natural world. In my favourite passage from *Fiesta*, the wounded narrator, Jake Barnes, retreats to San Sebastian in Spain following the theatrics of his vacation in Pamplona. Swimming out into the Mediterranean, we read:

> I undressed in one of the bath-cabins, crossed the narrow line of beach and went into the water. I swam out, trying to swim through the rollers, but having to dive sometimes. Then in the quiet water I turned and floated. Floating I saw only the sky, and felt the drop and lift of the swells. I swam back to the surf and coasted in, face down, on a big roller, then turned and swam, trying to keep in the trough and not have a wave break over me. It made me tired, swimming in the trough, and I turned and swam out to the raft. The water was buoyant and cold. It felt as though you could never sink.

What strikes me about this passage is the way the sea swallows our narrator, and that the pleasure for him is precisely in the dissolution of his identity. The sea is an escape, a retreat from his troubles with Lady Brett into a world where he can 'never sink'. Ironically, the moment Jake Barnes feels most alive is the moment in which he is not present as Jake Barnes – this remains true for most of Hemingway's characters – but is present as a mouthpiece for the sea. This seems similar to Tomas's experience in *The Unbearable Lightness of Being* when he has embraced his metaphysical homelessness and, unhitched from his past, made love to another woman. Both characters must lose themselves to find themselves.

Sadly, this dissolution of identity is only temporary, a drug that will not last. Towards the end of *Fiesta*, Barnes turns to drink, and throughout *The Unbearable Lightness of Being* Tomas suffers from a crushing guilt. Like all of us, they want, and need, weight, despite the fact that they find the blinding nature of light intoxicating.

As I sit here and watch the sun setting over Cape Town, I feel a similar process is at work within me. I am not here at all, but instead imagining myself as I might be. The landscape of the Cape Peninsula has become my light. I see myself walking beside you. We are wading out into the sea, our skin glistening and sparkling. Our bodies rise like tulips out of the spray. Whatever pain we have endured in the past is gone, lost in the roar of the waves. As Jake Barnes floated happily on the sea, I feel momentarily held up by the light and the landscape of this city, sustained by an illusion that will not let me sink.

I find it hard to imagine a city more suited to the play between destruction and creation than Cape Town. When Hangklip bows into the sea, its weight dissolving into light suggests a new beginning, a new lease on life. When, from a courtyard in the City Bowl, I see the edge of Table Mountain fade to blue, it is hard not to believe in a limitless future. And yet the mood that overtakes me in these moments has a dreamy, incandescent quality about it that I am learning to distrust. Strictly, I am not myself; I am at home, which is to say I am elsewhere. And finally I am coming to understand that like Kundera's moth, like Barnes and Tomas, all unable to extricate themselves from returning to the light, I return again and again to a city which merely offers the promise of home, in actuality widening the distance between my selves, leaving me nowhere.

My last day in the city, we drive to the bench on Tafelberg Road. It feels as if I am shuffling over to meet a tall, elegant relative. At the parking lot, you turn the car off and the sounds of crickets and songbirds beside the car grow louder.

From over the Lion's Rump appears a march of light, coloured liquid amber. I see a bank of cloud behind it. It looks as if a tidal wave is about to break and eddy back into the city.

For a long time we sit in the car, watching the clouds roll in. Though my hand is thrown across your shoulder, my mind is elsewhere. I stay perfectly, painfully still, until the Waterfront is hidden, the tall masts of the sailboats, hidden, the rusted cranes, hidden, only the mountain behind us present, and even that with something precarious about it, as if at any moment the rock might dissolve into air. From the City Bowl a pearl string of lights offers the distant promise of light. In the apartments above Long Street, windows are being closed; the hawkers are preparing for a night of wintry breath. And over the whole city a pause falls.

I'm sorry, you say. I hope you know that.

I know you're sorry. I'm to blame too, I sigh. We've gone through that.

You hold your hands in front of your face to hide your tears.

I don't want you to leave tomorrow with things being bad between us.

Neither do I, I reply. But you have to understand that I feel like something fundamental has been taken away from me. Like, I don't know, I was promised *more*. I shake my head in frustration. This is so hard to explain.

A set of headlights flash past, and two sets of greedy eyes, peering in at us. In the rear-view mirror I watch the red tail-lights of the car slowly fade. Once they have blinked out, Cape Town is again lost in the shroud of cloud and fog.

And so now what?

And now what? I repeat. Nothing. That's the whole point – don't you see? If I could leave you things would be easier. But I can't. I love you, you know that.

Yes, but now I'm worried that you *will* leave me.

No, I shake my head firmly. I'm not going anywhere.

Luke West, born in Canada, has lived on and off in Cape Town since the age of five. He graduated from New York University's Masters Programme in Creative Writing in May 2005. He currently teaches Expository Writing at NYU. His fiction, non-fiction and poetry have appeared in SA *Sports Illustrated*, *Carapace*, *Painted Bride Quarterly* and *The Harpweaver*.

Hedley Twidle and Sean Christie

Taxi on Main

Main Road, Cape Town begins at the Castle, curves around the base of Devil's Peak and then traces a line through the southern suburbs until it reaches the Indian Ocean. Here it bends right around the Muizenberg and follows the coastline all the way to Simon's Town. In the forty or so kilometres between these two original enclaves of European settlement at the Cape – the defensive pentagon of the Dutch East India Company and the naval base used by the British to provide safe anchorage from winter gales – it passes through areas so different that it is difficult to believe they could be called a single city.

What would a biography of Main Road reveal, charting its earliest beginnings as South Africa's first highway – the *wagen pad na t'bos* mentioned by Van Riebeeck in his journal of 1655 – to the congested, noisy transport artery it is today? This is a route – often neglected, much maligned – which leads through the scars of forced removals as well as lush imperial estates, via transplant museums, textile houses and crack dens, through student, vagrant and pensioner territories. Crossing rent gradients as dramatic as the slopes above it, Main Road takes in mall complexes and garden suburbs that soon give way to junk shops and wholesalers, passing both Immorality and Millionaires' Miles. It bypasses almost everything, including the corroded colonial promenades of the False Bay seaboard and the tidal swimming baths which exist on the sites of the rock pools used by *strandlopers* to trap fish more than five thousand years before Europeans arrived, as well as coloured beach huts, seafront amusements and ocean railways.

Perhaps tracing this buckled, scoliotic spine and all its cultural byways might provide a way of approaching the intangible but always intriguing question: how much does the spirit of a particular place at a particular time inform and shape the novels and poems written there, and how have writers in turn made Cape Town a place in the mind? Perhaps its oldest road might cut across the city's cultural history in unexpected ways, providing a map to locate those images that imaginations have snagged on over the centuries. Or at least a rough guide to the writers who have lived, worked, and been imprisoned or forcibly removed along this historical axis, once a buffer zone between rich and poor, between White and Coloured, now a space where all kinds of Africans find themselves mingling. And if the dialectic of mind and place is always an elusive one, the means of transport to be used for a preliminary survey is in no doubt:

Mowbray   Kaap   toe   Kaap   toe   Kyape   Town
RondeboschClaremontWynbeeeerrrrrrrg!

The shouts of the taximen provide the first map of Main Road, echoing under the corrugated iron arches of Cape Town's central taxi rank. By five am the Toyota Hi-Aces are revving in their queues – the Hot Stepper, the Dream Lover – as traders lay out pyramids of fruit and lug huge kitbags of merchandise up the steps from the rail station. More than the Castle just opposite, this open-air deck seems to be the start of Main today, perhaps even the focal point of this far-flung, disjointed city, if it can be said to have one at all.

At Bay 20, students, servants, shoppers, businessmen and even the odd intrepid tourist are herded into the vehicle – a rare link, or at least point of contact, between the split personalities of Cape Town: the First World city centre, a tourist and property agent paradise cradled by the mountain behind us, and the planned grids of the Flats, still illuminated in the dawn haze by massive floodlights. By six o'clock Lower Woodstock is bustling: there are long queues at the bank machines, smartly dressed women in head shawls waiting outside the metal grilles of the textile houses.

'Zhaun's, thank you … Caltex. Chippies. Next stop? Shoprite … second Engen … Groote Schuur.'

The doorman keeps up a running commentary of the waypoints where people board or descend, a mental map of the route extending all the way from the 'First stop in Woodstock? Let's talk about it … don't be shy' all the way to Wynberg, the end of this Main Road run. Under the Eastern Boulevard, there is a scuffed billboard showing a Toyota minibus juxtaposed with London and New York cabs. The slogan reads: 'To be a world famous taxi you have to outrun the competition.' But in fact South African minibuses have nothing to do with the quiet, insulated back-seat tours of a city offered by metered cabs. They are part of the much larger transport networks that serve the rapidly urbanising metropolises of the developing world: *matatus* in Kenya, *bakassi* in Khartoum or *públicos* in Puerto Rico, a ragged fleet of small buses and open-back trucks stretching from

Cape to Cairo to Kuala Lumpur.

The rush hour is still building as daylight gives shape to the inland escarpment visible to the left across the Flats where Main crosses the Settlers Way; to the right the various highways and boulevards leading into the city loop and curl around the slopes of Devil's Peak. The tourist authorities responsible for keeping up appearances regard this as the land gateway to the city: the roads converging below and the immense, angular rock walls above draw the eye towards the old icons of Cape Town up on the slopes: restored summer houses and the university campus; wildlife paddocks framed by stone pines; statues gazing into hinterlands; gardens and gables. From here, though, wedged four-deep inside the Rock of Ages, there is no recourse to natural splendour. The low roof of the vehicle blots out the spectacle of the mountain, fixing the gaze at street level: bucket shops, fried chicken outlets, exhaust fitters and the grey brutal slab of the new Groote Schuur hospital obscuring the graceful older building where the world's first heart transplant took place in December 1967.

In his 1997 meditation on place, *A Writer's Diary*, the poet and critic Stephen Watson quotes a friend from Paris who remarks that she could not really find Cape Town beautiful because 'unlike that European city, the South African one did not have its Baudelaire or Utrillo (the artist who had represented much of the arrondissement where she'd lived). Hence it had never been transformed into a place in the mind, the imagination. The beauty of the place thus remained on the level of the merely spectacular, the touristic.' Yet if you're sitting on a rumbling subwoofer, windows half-blocked by someone's monthly shopping, you are spared Cape Town's grand gestures and sweeping panoramas. The taxi screens out the sheer sense data of the topography which threatens to outdo any act of the descriptive imagination, rendering the mind blank, content just to gaze and remain silent, or fumbling in cliché and outdated shorthands – the Mother City, the Fairest Cape, the Tavern of the Seas.

The view from Main Road, then, is not the view from the sea, not the sleeping giant Adamastor in Canto V of Camoens's *Lusiads*, the sixteenth-century Portuguese epic in which generations of English poets found a ready-made receptacle for amorphous mythic outpourings. Nor is it the panorama offered from Robben Island – the 'patch of flatness on the sea's horizon' in Mtutuzeli Matshoba's 1979 cross-country journey to the Isle of Makana – to which latter-day pilgrims are dispatched every half-hour by high-speed ferry from the shopping wharves of the Waterfront. The view from Main is equally not of 'great spaces washed with sun' as seen from the Rhodes Memorial or Smuts Track, of imperial prospects and the geometries of segregation that followed in their wake traceable far below: group-area grids, heartless African autobahns, the ribbon of garden suburbs giving way to the dusty dormitory suburbs, box-like 'Mandela houses' and scrap-metal towns. *Langa, Nyanga, Guguletu, Khayelitsha.* Sun, Moon, Our Pride, New Home.

From these vantage points Cape Town emerges in stark historical relief, too easily becoming an entirely symbolic topography which invites the temptation of a different kind of spectacular, one which, as Njabulo Ndebele warned in the 1980s, can hijack the imaginations of writers at the expense of the ordinariness – the textures, the particulars – of individual lives. Yet as anyone who moves through it knows, a city is not a socio-economic survey or a problem to be solved. Like a novel or poem it is a place of overlapping rhythms, a world of sounds, private pleasures, short cuts and sensations. And as rush hour on the N2 reveals, with the bulk of its population shuttled between home and work each day, permanently in transit, the apartheid city – a city of division – was also a place of constant crossings: between languages, different behaviours, official roles and informal sectors. Hundreds of taxis are riding into town, burning along hard shoulders and empty bus lanes, overtaking commuter sedans three at a time, depositing their cargo on the slipways and then returning even faster to their local ranks. We tack across three lanes and brake violently to pick up more custom, the conductor herding those who need to change routes into his vehicle.

'*Yiza mama, yiza sisi* … Yes officer, *ons laai* … *Ons beweeg,* driver, *druk druk druk* …'

He switches lingos, fends off poachers and placates an unmarked police car all at the same time while the traffic swerves and bottlenecks around us. Slow progress through the Mowbray second-hand strip as he stops to woo more custom with a clipped whistle, jumps out for a salomie in the space of a red light, then shouts across to the shop assistants taking a cigarette break. Pulled over in the shaded grounds of University Estate, the crier leans out over the roof and pleads with the students trooping down the hill.

'Town girl? Town? *Kyape Town*? Obs? *Mowbray Kaap toe Kaap toe Kaaaaap!*' '*RondeboschClaremmontWynbeeeerg!*'

His insistent, distended syllables join all the others to form the signature tune of Main Road, simultaneously soundtrack and potted history. Obs, where in the 1820s the Board of Longitude in London commissioned an institution of similar size and standing to the Royal Observatory at Greenwich for mapping the stars of a new hemisphere, yet only managed a half-finished building that seemed to have been dropped from the sky in a barren wilderness called Slangkop. Mowbray, named, like the pork pies, after a rural English village by wishful nineteenth-century immigrants to plaster over the earlier title Drie Koppen, marking the place where the heads of three slaves were set on pikes.

Now little more than on-ramp linking Main Road to the stream of sedans curving around the contours of the mountain above, Woolsack Drive names the site of a lavish yet flawed attempt to give Cape Town a literary identity, a fascinating case study in the perils of both literary tourism and political dabbling. On the slopes here, the arch-imperialist Cecil Rhodes had his architectural right-hand man Herbert Baker build a 'home in the woods for poets and artists' where they could draw inspiration from the mountain. 'Through a tap, as it were,' wrote William Plomer in his satirical 1933 biography of the Colossus: 'Unfortunately, when turned on, the tap seems to have produced little but mountain mist and a few hiccups of patriotic fervour.' The Woolsack became a place for Rudyard Kipling, the most famous laureate of the British Empire, to 'hang his hat up', and he holidayed here with his family for almost a decade, reading the *Just So Stories* to his children in close proximity to large African fauna on the bizarre imperial estate, enjoying 'the colour, light, and half-oriental manners of the land' (*Something of Myself*, 1937). Yet even Kipling's most ardent admirers admit that he never penned the masterpiece his hero and patron was confidently expecting, that he could not create South Africa in the way he had British India. The Woolsack, it seems, was a writer's retreat contaminated by its nearness to power: Rhodes's mansion was just a short walk away, through 'a ravine set with hydrangeas, which in autumn ... were one solid packed blue river'.

From Main Road today you can only catch glimpses of the Groote Schuur homestead – a white flickering behind the fences and foliage of what is now the presidential compound of Thabo Mbeki. If you obtain security clearance and drive up to the front door, you reach a curiously eclectic piece of architecture, a local vernacular twisted by the hand of northern Europe into 'a misalliance of shapes and styles'. This verdict comes from a more reluctant participant in Rhodes's dreams, the narrator of Ann Harries's 1999 historical novel, *Manly Pursuits*. Professor Francis Wills, a reclusive Oxford don and ornithologist, is responsible for supervising the release of two hundred English songbirds into forests of the Groote Schuur estate, a fictionalised account of a real (but doomed) project that was part of Rhodes's drive to 'improve the amenities of the Cape' and transplant the sound of the English woodland to the tip of Africa before he died. For Wills the place is a museum piece: 'All teak and whitewash, flags and firearms, and a bath eight feet long hollowed from a slab of granite … As if building your house (twice) on the ruins of an old barn that stored the First Settlers' crops gives you some sort of sacred power – a mantle of belonging.'

Emerging around us as a strange mixture of giant ficus trees, student digs and tough old pensioners' blocks, Rondebosch was the earliest node of European settlement along Main Road after the Castle. A small, politically incorrect plaque tells us that 'In this vicinity on March 1 1657, nine free burghers took permanent title to land and became the first citizens of our country,' but the name preserves an unwritten history of aboriginal culture that goes back much further: *de ronde doorn bosjen* was probably a circular, kraal-like enclosure of thorn bushes built by the Khoikhoi herders for their cattle and fat-tailed sheep in the lee of the mountain. In his 2002 novel, *Islands*, Dan Sleigh one of many cultural archaeologists dislodging the myth of a Cape Dutch idyll which Rhodes and his ilk worked so successfully to invent, attempts to envisage the intrusion of settlement into the immemorial pastoral routes of the Goringhaicona, the Goringhaiqua and the Gorachouqua. His painstaking exploration of the Dutch East India Company archive provides a portrait of a place that was for much of its existence hardly an assured European beachhead but rather a 'makeshift, wavering, doubtful and extremely hungry community'. In the words of Noël Mostert's 1992 historical blockbuster, *Frontiers*, it was a backwater where the garden metaphor would never properly take root. In his *Daghregister,* Van Riebeeck describes how starving colonists were reduced to eating dead animals and begging succour from passing ships – a company report that is best approached as the diary of a man at his wits' end rather than the founding document of a city.

Today the Rondebosch Fountain is marooned on a traffic island, the drinking trough filled with rainwater, wrappers and chicken bones; the Liesbeek flows in a concrete canal that doubles as a laundry for modern urban nomads, while the Fountain Centre squats half-empty and ugly on the old village green, one of many graceless malls that line the route. Outside it, conductors fight over customers emerging from the Pick 'n Pay, each seizing an old woman by the elbow in a tug of war.

'This way Auntie, this way please, just give me the bags.'

We pull away from the fracas, speed up through Newlands, past armed-response men on cycles, and the brewery in league with sports stadium, get fully loaded in the crush of Claremont, then cruise through Kenilworth, where the road meanders a little for the first time. The taxi struggles up between the Edwardian mansions of Wynberg, then we rattle into the rank where onions are frying and an enormous *amakhu mashali* – queue marshal – sits on an upturned crate, checking off the vehicles as they load. Beyond the junk shops, bookies and medicine-man booths, the tar stretches onward through the suburb of Plumstead – nondescript, marginal, anonymous – where one writer in waiting spent listless days playing cricket with himself as a boy: Coetzee territory.

Distinguished Professor and Nobel Prize winner, John Maxwell Coetzee would seem to be the Master of Cape Town if ever there was one. Yet a realist depiction of the city remains tantalisingly absent from his books, its natural history and normally inescapable topography notable only by their absence. The difficulty in placing Coetzee's work is matched by his reluctance to explain it, a formidable reputation for shunning award ceremonies and interviews, a writing discipline intent on imagining things entirely on its own terms. Nevertheless, what might a circuit of 'Coetzeean' Cape Town take in, after the fashion of a township tour, those urban safaris to the Flats in private minibuses carefully managed by the Cape tourist board? The fringes of Site C, perhaps, where Mrs Curren watches vigilantes disguised in white scarves burning down shacks, or the Buitenkant flyover under which she collapses, her mouth pried open by street children in search of gold teeth. The gated apartments in Green Point where university lecturer David Lurie has his weekly appointment with the 'exotic' prostitute Soraya, or perhaps just the English Department of the University of Cape Town where Coetzee taught for many years, his pigeonhole lingering on even though he has long since left for Australia.

At the other end of Cecil Rhodes's baleful imperial axis, Naguib Mahfouz has made the alleys of the old Arab quarter, al-Gamaliyya, the heart of his Cairo trilogy. Fellow Nobel Prize winner Nadine Gordimer's Johannesburg has its own, bitterly realist poetry of blighted suburbia, corrugated iron towns and industrial residues. Yet even once the distanced worlds of Coetzee's early novels have resolved into something more recognisable as the Cape in *Life and Times of Michael K* (1983), trying to divine a notion of place in any traditional sense from his work is an impossible task. Responding to an interviewer's question about the precise coordinates of this archetypal wanderer's great anti-trek north from a menacing city of curfews and prison camps, Coetzee remarks that his fiction's geography is in no way trustworthy 'because I don't have much interest in, or can't seriously engage myself with, the kind of realism that takes pride in copying the "real" world'. While other authors have been at pains to chronicle and interpret modern South Africa for concerned onlookers, Coetzee's sparse, barbed-wire prose strips away the familiar signposts and shorthands by which the Cape is read to reveal a place at once clearer and more strange. Or if it does locate itself explicitly, it offers a portrait where this 'city prodigal of beauty, of beauties', as Lurie puts it, slyly resists, as does the literary work itself, all those ways in which it *ought* to be read.

Perhaps following one of the scenic drives taken by the redoubtable Mrs Curren in her Hillman – eager to burn the beauty of her surroundings into her mind's eye one last time before her death, confessing all to the deadpan vagrant Verceuil – Main Road now continues onward toward the coast. En route to Simon's Town on the upper highway, Breyten Breytenbach tried to avoid looking at the buildings of the notorious Pollsmoor Prison which he knew to be nestled amid vineyards and greenery just outside his field of vision in Tokai: 'It accompanies me like some dark peripheral image.' After two years of solitary confinement in Pretoria he was transferred here, his 1984 prison diaries recording an acutely sensitised mind set adrift and wandering in a maze of language, trying to reconstruct and recover an entire world from the small portion of mountain visible over the walls, yet haunted at every turn by a sense that its efforts would never make it out: 'Writing took on its pure shape, since it had no echo, no feedback, no evaluation, and perhaps ultimately no existence.'

The True Confessions of an Albino Terrorist is one of several minor classics of prison writing that have emerged from the Cape's fearsome penal archipelago. Athol Fugard's minimalist drama of the 1970s, *The Island,* and the chilling poetic economy of Dennis Brutus's 1968 *Letters to Martha* form a darker counterpoint to the struggle memoirs from Robben Island; Alex La Guma's short works blur the boundary between the cells of Roeland Street Jail and the ghetto beyond it; Albie Sachs's 1966 *Jail Diary* culminates in a euphoric victory lap from there through the city into the ocean. In Jeremy Cronin's celebrated 1983 poetry collection *Inside,* the experience of physical enclosure paradoxically unlocks an expansive lyricism; cooped up he remembers the 'Faraway city, there/with salt in its stones/under its windswept doek,' his mind playing over the geography of his Simon's Town childhood, its 'dockyard hooters on mornings of mackerel-green sea/that cast up sea-eggs, Argonauts, unexplained white rubber balloons./A soft sea full of cutting things, of sharktooth, barnacles and ultramarines.'

Reaching the coast, Main Road curves around Randlords' villas, small boat harbours and old gun emplacements to end here, where the *SAS Isandhlwana* and other hi-tech warships purchased in the government's latest arms deal lie at anchor and the different architectures grafted onto the Cape coastline spread around the yacht basin:

> *rhizomes*
> > *of Club Mykonos*
> > > *apartments*

> > *Cape*
> *Dutch gable*
> > *Fungi*

> > > *Floral*
> > *Filigrees*
> > *Of English iron*

in the words of Geoffrey Haresnape. Or perhaps Main Road ends slightly further on, where human settlement peters out at the edge of Cape Point Nature Reserve and sea air turns to cloud as it strikes the first swells of a continent starting. But for now, a quick turnaround into a vehicle with grotty, unpadded interior and a door pulled shut by a shoelace, the doorman staring with glazed eyes at the passing scenery that plays on an endless loop.

NEW FOREX PROBE. I'M NO GUILTY WHITE, SAYS MP. KINDERS WORD AL DOMMER. By mid-afternoon in a capsule full of fumes, the frenetic scenery of the Road somehow slowly unspools behind the window glass, punctuated by the cryptic clipped messages offered to the public by newspaper posters. Halaal butcheries and stacks of disconnected basins lurch by in the windows, with car seats on the pavements in Woodstock and the sound of *adhaan* from the mosques of Salt River. Passing through the intricate architecture of Muslim shop cloisters, for a moment it feels like a chowk in Old Delhi, or a north African medina. Department stores on the main drag promise lounge suites on hire purchase and 'lay-bye,' while to the right flicker narrow lanes leading off to the fisheries, mills and depots surrounding the Salt River railway works, once the country's biggest industrial area. 'Its shops are respectable, its lanes notorious,' wrote Richard Rive, struggling with the paradoxes of the Cape Town street scene in a short story from the 1965 collection *Quartet*: 'It is clean and dirty, modern and old-fashioned, plastic and enamel, with just a touch of crinoline and sedan chair. It contains bank managers and clerks, whores and pimps. Mosques and churches, Englishmen, Afrikaners, Coloureds, Moslems, Africans, Jews, gentiles, Germans, Greeks, Italians.' With the low helmet of the roof still in place, the urban fabric of the city centre is revealed for what it is: the high-rise filing cabinets, graph paper flats and cricket screens of the CBD, the ugly carapace of the Good Hope Centre below the cleared slopes of 'Cape Town's Hiroshima', as Rive called District Six.

Back at the taxi deck the rhythm of operations has shifted down a few gears. At its edge, where portable braiding salons and makeshift phone booths wait for custom, the view brings home how compact the City Bowl is: a dense knot of banks, cranes and all other human business cupped and constrained by immense heaves of quartzitic sandstone. In Johannesburg, the broadcasting towers, diamond-hard head offices and slag heaps all rise up from the Highveld to advertise an instant city whose reason for existence is crassly obvious yet also invisible. But in Cape Town the virtuoso geology denies the business district its usual assurance; the rock walls of the Graafwater Formation show up – starkly, continually – the errors and eyesores made by Cape Town's planners. 'I tried to imagine the place in a few years time,' says the narrator of André Brink's 1974 novel, *Looking on Darkness*, of the flattened working class tenements, 'With imposing white mansions in New-Cape Dutch, Pseudo-Corbusier, and Hottentot-Gothic.' In fact most of the area remained undeveloped, with only the churches, mosques and temples left standing as indicators of the false piety of the social engineers. Yet the architectural hybrids Brink foresaw have appeared in the vast mall and casino complexes on the Flats, stockades of faux-Tuscan columns and exotic Africana under closed-circuit surveillance. Perhaps the most fitting monument to Cape Town's brutal twentieth-century rearrangement is the Western Bypass, complete with unfinished outer viaducts dangling in the air, a memorial to an ideology of division so ambitious it achieved an almost total segregation between city and ocean.

As a way of remembering all those planned out of existence, the floor of the District Six Museum has become a reconstituted street grid on which one-time residents can inscribe their names and stories. Yet if popular memory can hardly escape a nostalgia that all but forgets the violent and desperate slum of La Guma's 1967 novella *A Walk in the Night*, perhaps another memorial is provided by the music of the Cape, particularly the distinctive sound of its jazz which, as Albie Sachs has written, bypasses, overwhelms, ignores oppression, establishes its own space. Abdullah Ibrahim has compared Cape Town's musical landscape to that of cities in the American south where jazz originated, a New Orleans-style mix of slaves, immigrants, Creoles, street funerals and carnivals. Ibrahim, as aficionados agree, is above all a storyteller, a musical raconteur who in famous standards like *Kramat*, *Tuan Guru*, *The Mountain* and *Mannenberg* outlines a sacred personal geography, his keyboard vamps and melodic turns of phrase as much a part of mapping the city as any author's. A reminder of how written accounts of the Cape will always leave out huge tracts of its experience, this blues for District Six – by turns dissonant, reverent, strident, joyful – seems the perfect metaphor for the improvisatory, ad hoc cultures that have always existed within designs of the planned city, and always will.

Returning from Wynberg for the last time, a driver from Somalia named Hassan takes time to point out the early evening sights.

'I've made my money for today; I'm driving for myself now. Hey look, you see the pro's coming out?'

There are lone figures in the pools of yellow light as we cruise through the Immorality Mile where the notorious apartheid act was brazenly flouted. Our guide explains that the combination of wide pavements and gated retirement homes creates a kind of no-man's-land ideal for prostitutes, and is sceptical about the government plans to 'recapitalise' the taxi industry, bringing it within the remit of the formal economy, regulating and replacing the battered Hi-Aces with a new fleet of custom-fitted buses.

'You can get a taxi every minute. I don't know what they want timetables for.'

Main Road, it seems, has always been an annoying glitch in the system for grand planners. First a frontier that stretched the resources of the Company, later an escape route for the moneyed classes which let the city follow in their wake, the sights, sounds and state of it a cause for complaint since written records began; a route of processions and protest, the site of surgical breakthroughs and equally outlandish cultural transplants. A place where chain gangs of /Xam prisoners were forced to labour, a transport corridor targeted by anti-apartheid saboteurs, the line of flight taken by Coetzee's Michael K, dragging his mother behind him in a home-made cart, hardly an unusual sight in this post-industrial, apocalyptic vision of the city: 'Stranger conveyances were emerging on the streets: shopping trolleys; tricycles with boxes over the rear axle; baskets mounted on pushcart undercarriages; crates on castors; barrows of all sizes.' Much of the literature of and about Cape Town today seems peopled by the fictional progeny of this holy innocent who evades both work camps and charity, yet pays close attention to plant life, stones and invertebrates, the shells and anemones in the rock pools at Sea Point: organisms that are anchored and complete unto themselves, that simultaneously build and are built into their own shelter.

Other, more recent writers, like the late K Sello Duiker in his *Thirteen Cents* (2000), have provided other visions of this city. But Main Road is still the way into the city taken by Zoë Wicomb's Coloured protagonist as she travels to an abortion clinic in a finely focused 1987 collection of linked stories, assured by her white boyfriend that 'You can't get lost in Cape Town'. It is also the route that brings in buses of revellers to an ANC rally at the end of her 2000 novel *David's Story*. Like much contemporary writing, it is a novel that reveals the process of South Africa's transition as painful, unpredictable, unpunctual. Yet for a brief moment, the people reclaim the city centre on a day that, the narrator realises, also commemorates James Joyce's linguistically dazzling pilgrimage through the Dublin of *Ulysses*: 'The sixteenth of June – Soweto Day – Youth Day – Bloomsday – Day of the Revolution of the Word – birthday of freedom.'

The hard-won lyricism of contemporary Cape poets offers another kind of imaginative freedom, recovering insights and ways of being that may have been submerged during times of acute political tension, logging details of light and landscape that emerge as analogues of a city in flux. For if on the one hand Cape Town is relentlessly divided by its history – with rich and poor, human settlement and natural beauty set permanently at odds – from day to day it appears as a place of shifting populations and weather systems off the ocean, a peninsula out on a limb at the tip of Africa which seems almost like a crucible for the social dynamics of a new century, and one that is producing every imaginable form of urban settlement.

Returning to Cape Town along the N2, the disgraced protagonist of Coetzee's post-apartheid novel watches while a child with a stick herds a stray cow off the road and into the shanty towns: 'Inexorably, he thinks, the country is coming to the city. Soon there will be cattle again on Rondebosch Common: soon history will have come full circle.'

And so, in a sense, has this taxi. We have arrived at the Deck for the last time. By now the smell of exhaust is worked deep into clothes, and there is an international film crew sealing off streets to one side – an everyday sight in Cape Town – no doubt using the backdrop to fill in for the Mediterranean, Sydney harbour or downtown Los Angeles. Most of the taxi stands are empty now, but lone vehicles are still operating, and will carry on late into the night.

'Five rand, okay? After-hours price.'

The last taxi of the day. The driver, fez-wearing, old and gentlemanly, says he is only in the business part-time. He waits at petrol forecourts, angling for customers, meanders down back alleys until people start complaining about how late it is, that they have paid double fare, that they want to get home now.

Hedley Twidle was born in 1980, grew up in Pofadder and Potchefstroom, and studied at the universities of Oxford and York. He now lives between Cape Town and Edinburgh. He is currently researching a book entitled *Main Road*, an attempt to chart the course of the oldest transport artery in South Africa, and in the process draw a literary map of the Cape Peninsula.

Sean Christie was born in Zimbabwe, has lived in Britain, America, Taiwan and now works as a barman in Vredehoek, Cape Town. He has written television scripts and newspaper articles and is currently occupied with a novel inspired by the exhumation of slave bones from Prestwich Place.

Nkululeko Mabandla

The Mist, the Wind, and the Two Oceans

I

Far in the recesses of my memory is a childhood memory – one of my more lucid childhood memories, that is. It dates way back to the Seventies, when Percy Sledge came to town. This is by no means my first memory of Cape Town, what with the city being my maternal grandparents' home and all. It's just that this memory, by some curious force of nature or some curious element of memory preservation, is forever embedded in my consciousness and remains crisp even today.

In the Seventies, just like now, the local airwaves were inundated with American music; so Percy Sledge, of the monster hit *When a Man Loves a Woman*, was big news down here. This was the time of the Afro, American pop culture, American cars. This was pre-sanctions, before the cultural boycott days. All things American like the Valiant, the Buick and the Ford Fairmont were big stuff in the townships. An even more widely imported variety of this pop culture was the music. Soul music was a big thing back then, huge in fact, and one could find no better exponent of the genre than Percy.

Of course Cape Town back then was a totally different place altogether. Besides work and some shopping and perhaps an occasional movie or concert here and there, there really wasn't much interaction between town and township. If you were from the township, after hours you were an alien; you had to make sure to catch the last train of the afternoon and disappear; you had no business being in the city. You could end up in jail if you were unlucky enough to be caught by some cantankerous official or policeman. You always saw long lines of people coming out of Nyanga station in the afternoon just before sunset. You would see this endless procession, like an ant colony, of all those who caught the last choo-choo out of town.

There is a buzz in Cape Town when important events are imminent. I don't know whether this is due to its relative smallness or the fact that Cape Town is at the bottom end on the map of South Africa, but this has been so ever since I can remember. At any rate, we knew something special was afoot, we felt it; a mood of great anticipation hung heavily in the township air. As young as we were back then, we knew Percy's song, we felt its quaint romanticism as only prepubescent boys could. And so, when he came a-calling, we took more than passing notice.

It was the festive season and everywhere one went people were talking of the coming show. Such was the excitement that we got caught up in it as well. This impending visit by an international superstar had transformed us overnight into knowledgeable and sophisticated citizens of the world.

Merely being enveloped by this effervescence had somehow made a difference to our mundane childhood existence. We never once thought we were too young to go to the show.

You can well imagine, then, our disappointment when we found out that we were. Something had to be done to assuage our hurt feelings. As luck would have it, there was one other attraction almost as thrilling as an evening with Percy Sledge: 'the lights'. It was an annual ritual every December to go to the city in the evenings to view the festive lighting and decorations – one of the few times we children would go into the city. We would know this special day long in advance; for days we would talk of nothing else. (In those years there were far fewer cars in the township. So you can imagine what a mission it was getting to the city, whether for a show or to see those lights.) But the sight of them would warm the cockles of our young hearts as we craned our young necks from the inside of the kombi, trying to catch a glimpse of the luminous, multicoloured spectacle.

December is a special month all over the world because of Christmas. But to us kids the month was mostly associated with the long summer break we would have from school, the presents and the new clothes we would get for Christmas, and of course False Bay's Mnandi beach for Boxing Day and New Year's. The disappointment of missing out on Percy was soon forgotten. And I would presume to say the Seventies were quite memorable – quite hip actually – to any fun-loving boy of my generation, this being the time of Oxford bags, the Chopper bicycle, and Motown. If you were of the sporting kind as well, the Seventies were even more fun. These being pre-TV times, the indestructible PM10 battery put out in the sun to charge, and the eventual gathering around the old beat-up transistor radio listening to feats of sporting greats like Pelé and Gordon Banks, Blue Angel Sibaca and Happyboy Mgxaji, the great Frik du Preez and Colin Meads. I remember an All Blacks tour at the time, when we gathered around this selfsame transistor radio chanting 'miss, miss, miss …' as 'Oom' Frik readied himself for a goal kick.

The Seventies for us young boys were about fashion, sport, music, and the beautiful American model Marcia Turner. This was of course a decade when we were still young and carefree – before Hector Peterson, our peer, became a martyr of the liberation struggle. From then onwards we were never young boys again. We grew up quickly, almost overnight.

II

There is a frustrating intransigence about Cape Town towards transformation and attitude change – a maddening provinciality akin to backwardness or 'bumpkinism'. Comparatively speaking, Cape Town is probably last among the great cities of the world when it comes to integration. This is somewhat surprising when one takes into account that of all South African cities, Cape Town has long been regarded as a bastion of liberalism. In a country of so many cultures like South Africa, there are still very few cross-cultural exchanges on any level, grass-roots or otherwise, in this city; people pretty much keep to themselves. It can only happen in Cape Town that when homeless black people whose shacks have burnt down are being housed in a vacant building, the local Coloured community gets its knickers in a knot – and this ten years into our democracy.

But this backwardness has long been a special characteristic of Cape Town. In the black townships, for instance, anyone from beyond the urban borders was always referred to as 'emaXhoseni' (from Xhosa country); they were considered less sophisticated and streetwise, and were ostracised even by people with whom they shared the same culture and language. Again, the Western Cape and Cape Town have the dubious reputation of being the only province and city to have voted for the old National Party in the first democratic elections. (Legend has it that after the 1994 elections all the rich *verkrampte* whites fled from the other provinces to Perth or to Cape Town, where they set about hiking property prices and hotel and restaurant charges in order to keep everyone out, especially the 'previously disadvantaged'.) There is also the belief that Cape Town has been better serviced and functions much more efficiently than the other metros because of this. Needless to say, a fallacy. Walking through the centre of town one Saturday afternoon, I was struck by how much Cape Town is like any other South African city. Even in the Golden Acre, on that afternoon, either the doors were locked or the escalators were switched off.

Cape Town is not only known for its reactionary politics; some of the more militant struggles were fought here. Among these were the first removal of Africans from District Six in 1901, resistance to the Native Affairs Act of 1920, and resistance to the forced removals of Ndabeni in the 1920s, which resulted in the establishment of Langa as the first African township. You also had great political struggles in places like Elsies River, Bonteheuwel and Guguletu. And of course not every white person is rich and *verkrampte*. Some of the most humane, generous and gracious people come from this section of the population as well. The examples are many.

Today Cape Town has blossomed into a much more welcoming city, becoming a melting pot of multicultural diversity. It is home to an ever-increasing number of languages and dialects. Immigration, as in Australia and the United States, has also had a positive impact. Multiculturalism is everywhere. In Cape Town today you can eat anything from bobotie to couscous, from crocodile steak to *umbengo* (township braais).

You can listen to *klopse* and see West African sculpture.

In fact, Cape Town is more cosmopolitan and much bigger than ever before. People from as far afield as Mali and Nigeria, Botswana, KwaZulu-Natal, Somalia and Joburg – you find them all in this city nowadays. If one were to subvert the lyrics of that old King Kong classic, one could sing: 'Cape Town is bigger than King Kong ... Cape Town is bigger than King Kong.' Walking through the central business district, Cape Town station, Greenmarket Square, one can see that it has become a much more exciting, colourful city. It's a relaxed, good-time place. The saying goes, you first make your money elsewhere and come retire in Cape Town; life here is much more laid-back, the people friendly, easygoing. In the Golden Acre once more, the escalators are switched off. On seeing this, a young man decides to run up one of them. He stumbles, almost falls. He holds on to the escalator for balance and stays like that for a short while. 'You see, from trying to be fast,' someone remarks good-naturedly. The young man laughs self-consciously. 'I'm drunk,' he says.

That exchange could not have summed up better the good nature and good humour of people in Cape Town. Down at the station, the ticket booths are deserted and appear to have been closed a while. My friend from Durban is worried: no one is selling tickets; what if she's required to produce a ticket further on? We ask the station guards, the only people with a semblance of authority in sight. They say it is okay, no one will ask for a ticket. We wonder if this is a usual occurrence. Yes, it happens sometimes, they say. And we wonder if this is that Cape Town thing again – laid-back, relaxed, and with its sense of all-in-good-time? (Or, more alarmingly, we wonder if it's that post-independence syndrome of '*Angola libre, o povo relaxao*' – Angola is free; the people shall relax.) We hope and pray nothing goes amiss and my friend boards the train. This being a Saturday afternoon, a warm and sunny one at that, I suppose everyone just wanted to knock off early …

The other striking thing about this city is, no matter which side you approach it from, you always see the mountain. Looking up, you always see Lion's Head in the background – majestic Lion's Head, imposing and aloof, as if standing guard, a sentinel, over the coastline and the city. Suddenly it strikes you that Cape Town is where it all started. You wonder what stories some king on top of the hill would tell; for surely he must have seen the three ships that so altered the course of history back in 1652. And just as surely as he sees the merchant ships coming in and out of the Waterfront today, he would have seen those boats bringing Nelson Mandela from the Island to the mainland.

It was here, in this city that with its slave history evokes so strong a sense of oppression, that Nelson Mandela took his first steps to freedom. And now one gets a sense of elation from knowing that that past is well and truly gone, never to return. You get a sense of deep satisfaction knowing that *sibuyele eDistrict Six* (we are back in District Six), as the song *District Six* by Hugh Masekela has it. And I still like 'the lights'. Soft yet colourful, the whole of Adderley Street is transformed into one long, brilliant avenue. One can't help being seduced by them even now. For me, with the combination of festive season lights, Adderley Street and its bustling night market, its sounds and smells – toy stalls and food stalls, dried figs, and one vendor crying 'lovely peaches', another 'ten rand flowers' – there can be very few Cape Town experiences to surpass this one.

Still, Cape Town remains a city of contrasts and paradoxes, of mesmerising physical beauty and grandeur on the one hand and abject poverty and hopelessness on the other. And these side by side too. Consider this image: it's morning on the Sea Point promenade where a group of bergies sit sunning themselves in the early sun while others trudge along, dragging shopping carts loaded to the brim with their worldly goods. All around them men and women in their fashionable sporting gear are power-walking, exercising their dogs, talking on cellphones, or jogging by with earphones plugged into their ears.

As I make my way down Main Road, I see a group of construction workers in their paint- and cement-crusted work clothes. Others sit spreadcagled on the pavement, eating – always a loaf of white bread and coke or Tropika juice. There's a lull in the work, they talk animatedly, cracking jokes, complaining about the Lotto; how one never wins it. (There must be something underhand about this, they say.) They come from diverse places, Nyanga, Joburg, Ntabankulu and Gatyana. And I'm reminded of the guy I saw earlier this morning, eyes squinting, glimmering, sad, his brow furrowed in utter despair, looking at these construction workers as they go about their chores. He must be looking for work, I think. (This is how most casual work is found in the city. You go door to door, stand by the side of the road and also hang around construction sites.) You can always identify somebody who woke up early in the morning to go and line up for work in town. It's something to do with the clothes; somehow the clothes are always out of place. They also have that hungry look about them; and there's always a plastic bag containing their particulars and certificates.

There's a lot of construction going up all over the city. Life must be good for construction workers; in fact the construction industry must be having a ball. The local economy must be very healthy indeed. This is always reassuring. And then Cape Town holds great promise for many people. Like Gerald, the 'entrepreneur'. If you say no to the Seiko watch, he shows you Ray-Ban sunglasses and then Hugo Boss Eau de Toilette. If you still say no, he cuts his price from one hundred and twenty rand to sixty rand. He doesn't give up. 'I've been selling these goods since yesterday,' he says. 'The trouble is people want to pay twenty for them.' He's from Korsten originally, in Port Elizabeth, and he's trying to raise money for the ticket back home. This is not a good place, he says. 'I don't have a place to stay, perhaps you have two rand for me, to buy food?' The irony of the situation is inescapable. Here is a man selling all this expensive stuff and he doesn't have two rand.

You wonder if he's telling you the truth. You wonder how he ended up like this. In the past, helping someone was no big deal. In countless stories by the fire, our grandmothers told us stories of the good old days; when there were no orphans and homeless; when no one ate from rubbish dumps; when people were especially kind to strangers and would prevail upon them to spend the night. When they would go out of their way to make others feel at home and would even slaughter their last chicken for supper and for provision for the road. You wonder what happened to those days. You wonder what happened to the principle of *ubuntu*. You also wonder if Gerald is not just some con artist selling you a sob story. You wonder too if we've become more sceptical. At the same time you feel great empathy towards those less privileged. You always wonder what it would be like to be so hungry. Would there be someone out there kind enough to give you bread? There's always a gnawing thought at the back of your mind, that it could easily be you. That's the reality of our times, a difficult trust born out of our bad past.

III

The skies are grey and in part a clear blue, almost like the heavens are divided into two. It's a funny day, muggy, and all of a sudden a cool breeze. Winter weather again: it rained and the wind howled bitterly overnight, another cold front on the way – how uncharacteristic for this time of the year. It seems Cape Town weather has been changing steadily over the years; there's even thunder and lightning in the city nowadays; seasons are no longer what they used to be. Almost each year there's a shortage of rain. We are still in the grip of El Niño, some say. Water restrictions have become a yearly occurrence. The winds and the rains have become much more unpredictable.

Cape Town rain comes when least expected, an icy, unrelenting downpour that can go on for days, flooding roads and washing shacks away, but also filling dams and making the parks green overnight. It's a magical rain. And then there're those other winds, gale-force, the berg winds and southeasters. Then the telephone wires sing, a mournful and melancholy tune. There's sand in your eyes, stinging your face like an army of angry wasps, turning the streets brown and dusty, emptying pavement bins, spraying litter all over the place, felling trees and blowing roofs away. Everyone walks with faces aligned to one side, as if about to keel over – as if a huge invisible hand is firmly placed on their backs, pushing them, hurrying them along. Yes, there's something unique about the climate and weather in Cape Town, and the winds and the storms are part of its legend.

Sometimes you see the moon during the day, a white ball hanging over the ocean. Beyond the harbour, the sea is like no other, sometimes green, sometimes blue, but clear, translucent, the waves whiter than white. I don't know whether it's a two-oceans phenomenon, but I've never noticed green water like this anywhere else. I remember once, on the stretch between Oudekraal and Llandudno, I remarked on this to a friend. 'What colour is the water?' I asked this beautiful girl. She looked at me like she had not heard. So I repeated my question. She looked at me quizzically – you know, as if I was talking nonsense – and replied: 'It's blue.'

The morning has become cloudy, misty, the waves are first undulating in slow motion, then hissing, before they crash against the rocks. A light breeze puts a spray to your face as you walk along the promenade in Sea Point. The coastline is in silhouette, the clouds and mist create an illusion of a smoky blue and white mountain range. Outlined against this are two sailing boats. A medium-sized cargo vessel chugs along from west to east, from the direction of Camps Bay to the V&A, towards the docks.

The city is sure to disgorge its other cargo, of the human variety, as well. They will come out in the evening, enticed by those bright and shining lights of Cape Town. Perhaps some will end up in Long Street – Long Street with its motley collection of shops, restaurants, bookshops, backpackers' lodges, cafés and art shops. All thrown together and mixed up with office and residential space. Serious and businesslike during the day, in the evening it's transformed into one hip and vibrant hang-out. You can dance all night on Long Street. The smell of food, the music from both sides of the street – it's a young street, a street for students, an all-ages street, a street for Australians, Germans, Moroccans. It's like a miniature of Tijuana Avenue.

I wonder what Percy Sledge would think. Would he kneel down and kiss the ground, happy to be back in the Mother City, happy to be in the Motherland? Would he go out on Long Street or would he prefer to go for a beer or two and perhaps some 'barbeque' in the townships? There are definitely many more cars in the township now; driving down the N1 is not for the faint-hearted. This applies both to the 'cockroaches' (the many hazardous, unroadworthy sedan taxis) and to the beautiful girls. As the old isiXhosa choral song has it: 'I have seen beautiful girls and I have seen a beautiful world in Cape Town.' So, would 'ou Percy' like to experience a little bit of that 'soul, man' at places like Popza's, Mzoli's and Tiger's? Where there's fun and laughter and talk aplenty – of service delivery and difficult bosses, of current affairs and the latest sporting news, of Bafana Bafana, the Bokke and the Proteas, of Chiefs and Pirates and of 'broad bases' (the new elite) and BEE (black economic empowerment)? Who's bought which wine farm and so on? Talk of the latest TV advert and how ridiculous or how 'sharp' it is? Yes, they'll talk of the latest celebrity, music star, TV star; they'll dance and listen to music. Some will go home after a short while, some will stay far into the night, until the money runs out and they can't get any more credit from the owner. (He's tired by now, his patience has been tested enough by those who can't hold their liquor or keep their hands from wandering, upsetting all the other, paying customers.)

Would he want to hear all this or would he just be glad that his brethren have drawn back from the precipice, drawn closer to the promised land – 'the miracle', as the outside world likes to call it? Would he also tell us why, those years ago, he chose to come to South Africa when many of his counterparts chose not to? He would find many of his brothers and sisters much more affluent than the last time he was in these parts. He would find some in Parliament and government and the corporate world. But he would also find most of his brothers and sisters in abject poverty still.

I wonder what Percy Sledge would think right now. It's turned into a beautiful afternoon, bright and shiny, sunlit. A few white clouds dot the clear blue sky as if painted upon it by some lazy painter – as if daubed nonchalantly yet perfectly by some invisible heavenly hand. I smell the sea from my bedroom (I've always liked the smell of the sea, so heady, salty, so intoxicating – a drug of sorts). I see the Atlantic as it merges with the sky into one endless blue and white expanse. A few birds chirp and flap playfully at indeterminate intervals. Black-winged with dusty brown chests – I don't know a whole lot 'bout them bird names, least of all in English. (I know few bird names in any language, period.) I think it's going to rain. These birds come before the rain. We call them *inkonjane* in isiXhosa. Would that be a swallow in English?

Yes, Cape Town is not so strange any more. It feels good to stand tall like my father did on Table Mountain, in that old black and white photo of my childhood memories. It feels good to own it and belong to it. It feels good to call it home, so nice to savour the sights and scents of Cape Town at all times, day and night, without having to rush to catch the last afternoon train. Seeing me come out of the house, a Coloured man, passing by, raises his fist and silently mouths '*Amandla!*' It starts to rain. It's a monkey's wedding, they call this rain, and it's quickly over. And now a rainbow straddles land and sea, like a huge rasta-coloured arch.

Nkululeko Mabandla, writer, actor, director and former free-dom fighter, grew up in Umtata. He went into exile at the age of seventeen and lived, worked and studied in Zimbabwe, Botswana, Angola, Mozambique, Lesotho, East Germany, Yugoslavia, Sweden and the United States before returning to South Africa in the 1990s. He's worked as an actor, a director of industrial theatre productions, and a writer of TV dramas, and he has completed the first translation of Chekhov's *Three Sisters* into isiXhosa.

Justin Cartwright

The Lie of the Land

I went to boarding school in Cape Town from the age of eight until the age of seventeen. This involved a long train journey, second class, to and from Johannesburg eight times a year, and a fairly brutal regime of cold showers, bullying, beating and rugby. And the food was awful.

From my dormitory in the junior school I could see the mountain rising like a Gothic cathedral. Sometimes it would be running with water, sometimes it would be pulsing with heat. Even now from the Rondebosch direction, every rock and kloof and peak is familiar to me. At night we could hear the lions roaring from the zoo – they, like me, no doubt wishing to be somewhere else. Like many provincials, I was dying to get away to where the action was.

The mountain came in my mind to stand for everything I loathed about Cape Town, a feeling which persisted until well into my forties. Where other people saw an astonishing natural phenomenon, I saw a kind of illusion, a dull little town given false glamour by the mountain. The most exciting moment of my school career, but also a little scary, was when a schoolboy called Philip Kgosana led a march into Cape Town and for a day or two the bourgeoisie trembled. There was nothing to match the ineffable smugness of Capetonians of the old school. How I longed to see them turned out.

Yet my family was the epitome of the bourgeois. My ancestor, Sampson Cartwright, arrived in the Cape in about 1850. His son, or grandson, became a merchant by marriage. A corner of Adderley Street is named after our family store. Last year, going into the *Argus* archive, I gave my name, and an elderly man asked me if I was anything to do with Fletcher & Cartwright's. I felt a strange pride in being the descendant of the man who sold it in order to become an actor. It did him no good: he died of yellow fever on his first tour.

I remember JM Coetzee writing somewhere about the enervating effects of the Cape wind which my godfather, Lawrence Green, routinely referred to in his books as the Cape Doctor. Long terms at Bishops, playing all manner of sports in the Cape Doctor, or trying to swim at Muizenberg – actually a little up the coast at 'Christian Beach', shamefully a reference to the fact that Muizenberg had a small but heroic Jewish population – in the teeth of the same Cape Doctor, gave me the feeling that Cape Town was bleached, scoured by the wind. So when I went in the middle Sixties to live in England, I had almost no desire to see Cape Town again.

The point of this story so far is not to take an easy ramble through the Freudian hinterland, but to try to explore something which has always fascinated me, the meaning of landscape. Recently I have been writing about Germany and reading – in translation – a few pre-war memoirs which always include references to *Landschaft*. Simon Schama has investigated the relation of landscape to national identity and landscape as the repository or the origin of essential national characteristics. The forest looms very large in Norse and Germanic mythology. Robert Hughes, in *The Fatal Shore*, described very clearly and, for a South African, significantly, the way that the first English settlers and transportees in Australia regarded the landscape. Essentially, they loathed it. It was dry, it was contorted, it was unfamiliar and it was inhabited by revolting and deformed creatures. It took at least a century for these settlers to rid themselves of the idea that the ideal landscape was the landscape of Europe, and specifically England.

In our lavatory in Johannesburg – red-cement-floored, very cool – we had a calendar which had a picture of Mad Ludwig's Neuschwanstein, and this seemed to me as a small boy utterly magical. Anyway, it's clearly part of the colonial experience to rid oneself of the longing for the old homeland, which Germans call *Heimat*. If you look at Afrikaner landscape paintings, Pierneef for example, you will see very early on that the homestead, nestling under an unmistakably African mountain, which is often cloaked in a kind of swirlingly numinous cloud, represents civilisation. This landscape is hostile, and must be tamed. The early painters of the American west, heavily influenced by the idea of the sublime, regarded the landscape with a sort of trepidation; it was magnificent but frightening. Where the Alps had largely been ignored as a font of beauty and significance, all this changed with the arrival of Ruskin and his chums, who saw towering mountains in quasi-religious terms, the triumph of feeling, a sort of tonic for the spirit.

So to Cape Town. The strange thing about Cape Town is that it is seen – among white people – as a kind of antidote to Africa. There are those in Gauteng who claim to love the bush and feel themselves wonderfully renewed when they go there, but there is also a substantial number of white people who see Cape Town as the last bastion of certain values. For a start, the landscape is utterly different. And it is perfectly possible in Cape Town to ignore the fact that one is in Africa. I remember at school being told that Cape Town had a Mediterranean climate, and assuming from that that it was a classier kind of climate, more refined, more classical, less turbulent. Africans of my acquaintance, few in number admittedly, seem to prefer Johannesburg to Cape Town. I would guess that it is precisely the reasons that white people give for liking Cape Town that put these Africans off: they feel that they have strayed into an alien and somehow hostile environment.

While I was at school I developed for the above-mentioned reasons an aversion to Cape Town. I, too, preferred Johannesburg with its sprawling suburbs, comparatively open veld and somehow, for those of us in the privileged north, the sense of space. I can't say that I was a lover of landscape as such, but somehow the Transvaal came in my mind to stand for happiness and freedom, and the Cape for a cramped and moderate unhappiness. I didn't realise it then, but landscape is an entirely artificial construct. For the Masai, I discovered when researching for my novel *Masai Dreaming*, landscape only has significance in relation to cattle. Hills are described in terms of cattle colouring; to become engaged is to become heifers; and to ask for mercy is to use the term 'green grass'. So animal husbandry informs the Masai's sense of landscape. And recently I discovered from Marguerite Poland's wonderful book that Nguni cattle were traditionally described in terms of objects and animals and topography. The point is that we construct our sense of landscape according to our needs or longings, not according to some natural order which will enlighten us or make us more sensible to the higher emotions, essentially the romantic idea.

For the last ten years or so I have been holidaying in Cape Town. Every time I arrive I am astounded by the landscape. I smell the fynbos, and feel my spirits raised. Since my schooldays I have completed a volte-face in this respect at least. In those days arriving at Rondebosch station after a thirty-six hour train journey, I was utterly dispirited. The mountain, which I regarded with a kind of indifference, I see now as miraculous, rising right out of the city, falling into the sea, providing, within minutes, peace or pounding beaches (I came very close to drowning at Llandudno two years ago) and the genuine sense that landscape can be a refuge from more pressing concerns. But even on holiday I feel the weight of the shacks on the Flats very heavily, as though my enjoyment must have been bought in some way by others' misery, by others having to get up at five in the morning on a winter's day, to leave a shack and look for work, or go from that shack to some poorly paid job, often at risk of mugging or murder. To see young men hunkering by the roadside in Hout Bay waiting for work before I pop into La Cuccina for an Italian coffee is an irony I can hardly cope with, although – you are probably, and justifiably, sneering – I do. I also head very quickly to Cape Point and attempt to catch crayfish, or make a braai, neither very successfully, in response to some sense of rightness. This is, after all, my *Heimat*, and I want to enter fully into it. It's a sort of invitation to feel at home and at ease. I believe, although I know it is nonsense, that it has significance for me. This is the romantic fallacy.

Cape Town likes to call itself the Mother City, or as my godfather used to say, the Tavern of the Seas, and it is undoubtedly a unique place, but the history which it is mother to is being relentlessly scrutinised and revised. The things that the tourist and the Capetonian treasure are – I sense – under threat from poverty, unemployment, and increased expectations. What the tourist likes about Cape Town – what I like about Cape Town – are all the things which have little or no relevance to the masses grouped outside town in their shacks, who see only an opportunity, however remote, to improve their lives, rather than to gratify their sense of the aesthetic or quasi-spiritual. To them the Kirstenbosch concerts, the drive down past Misty Cliffs, the infinite walks on the mountain, the vineyards of Constantia, the elegant hotels, the lingering sense of a colonial town, all these things are almost never going to figure in their landscape, which is mean, windswept and deprived. The army of occupation is at the gates, and yet still we continue our journey of self-exploration through the old standbys of landscape, fynbos, surf and mountain.

A few years ago South Africa believed that out of apartheid something wonderful would inevitably arise. Culture was supposed to be one of the vehicles for this change, as if it could be pressed into service for the benefit of the New South Africa. At the time I was sceptical: culture is often what small nations, the Welsh or the Catalans and now the Afrikaners, fall back on when they want to stress their differences or when they feel threatened by a majority. I can't avoid the sense that post-apartheid South Africa is still struggling with its sense of itself, ducking behind self-serving notions of the Rainbow Nation, while avoiding the real issue, namely that South Africa is a land where – and I could easily but disingenuously fall back on the evils of apartheid here – two or more nations live within the same borders but do not share some important conceptions. I remember well, at the time of President Mandela's inauguration, the organiser of the celebrations, Welcome Msomi, telling me that he was going to cut down 'the bushes' at the Union Buildings to make way for the stages. These bushes were a national collection of aloes, lending the Herbert Baker-designed building its strange appearance of English vernacular set in a pioneering landscape, aloes being a symbol of Afrikaner struggle. As I said at the time, one man's bushes are another man's landscape.

Cape Town is not waiting for my verdict, but I see in Cape Town the sharpest clash of culture and self-image in all of South Africa. Cape Town to some is one of the most startlingly beautiful places on earth, with its own unique atmosphere of colonial and Creole, a sort of haven from Africa; to others it is a smug and small-minded place, desperately unaware of its modest position in the firmament. I often think about this kind of thing on holiday as I stare out to sea hoping to see a Southern Right whale. Last year one breached just off the beach, its enormous tail flapping. It was signalling to me, but the message was unclear. Perhaps it was waving goodbye.

Justin Cartwright was born in South Africa and educated in the United States and at Oxford University. His novels include Look At It This Way, Interior, Masai Dreaming, In Every Face I Meet, **which was shortlisted for the Booker Prize,** Leading The Cheers, **which won the Whitbread Novel Award,** Half In Love, **the acclaimed** White Lightning **and his latest,** The Promise Of Happiness, **winner of the Hawthornden Prize for Literature in 2005. He lives in north London with his wife and, occasionally, with his two sons.**

Stephen Watson

Afterword to a City

I

You meet them even now: the psychiatrist long domiciled in London; the schoolteacher from Toronto; the child, now adult, of parents who emigrated to Australia in the 1980s. They left Cape Town years ago and for various reasons, all of them plausible, understandable. They have long since become a part of the great global and globalising diaspora of English-speaking peoples. They have prospered in their adopted countries, become acculturated, long since taken out citizenship. Even their accents might now carry the traces of other inflections, other tongues.

And yet whenever you should speak to them, and the many like them, the evidence is unmistakable: even after twenty years in Hampstead, north London, or London, Ontario, there appears something far-flung, lonely, lost about their lives. Even the calmness of the country where they now live seems a further form of loneliness, part of a moat of isolation that has dug itself around them.

In fact they are members of another phenomenon no less global: that of people who no longer have a place, who no longer know where they best belong. They have left one country never to find another that they might call their own. Their homes, however comfortable, remain the approximations of a home. They might recognise the force of some further words of Camus – 'a man who can feel his link with one country ... who knows that there is always a place where his heart will find its resting place already owns many certainties' – but their own hearts register this security only by its absence.

Like exiles of all times, they know also, instinctively, why the act of homecoming, whether it be that of Odysseus to Ithaka or Nick Adams to the upper reaches of Michigan and its Big Two-Hearted River, is always synonymous with peace and the rediscovery of peace. But they do not know this peace, or its healing properties. They know that a feeling for a place – that feeling that makes it a home – is one of the few consolations in life on earth that really do console; and that such things operate in genuine commutation of the sentence under which human beings are ordinarily condemned to live: the condition of being temporary, resident aliens all. But they know this only by default.

All this they understand only too well. And they know it all the more because there is something about the city they left long ago – so the evidence of their lives, of their every word, underlines – which suggests that they have never gotten over it. There is something about Cape Town – so one recognises afresh, as they talk on – which induces a homesickness the pure force of which is almost intimidating in its longing.

II

A person's first place in the world commonly has more barbs than a fishhook; it has a thousand ways of getting under the skin and staying there. But in the case of Cape Town, quite apart from the beauty that it possesses and that might well plague the memory of anyone once parted from it, there are a number of other features which work to embed themselves in the minds and hearts of those who have once lived here, seldom to be extracted.

It is a place remarkable not least for that which is also most hackneyed about it. Sydney finds its centre in a harbour bridge or Jørn Utzon's opera house; London in a cathedral. Cape Town, by contrast, is a city remarkable for having a mountain – in fact a chain of mountains – in the middle of it.

From almost any street in the city one need only raise one's head to see, there at the far end, the container harbour, the ships at their moorings. And one hardly need turn to find, at the other, a mountain docked like a liner from another planet. It has emerged from a world which underlies everything, the universe of rock and stone. Those who are privileged to live in this city inhabit a landscape the bones of which are everywhere exposed, naked to the eye, in the more than five hundred million years of granite, sandstone, slate and mudstone which is Table Mountain. They are close neighbours, first and foremost, to geology – that which acts, as the contemporary palaeontologist Richard Fortey has written, 'as a kind of collective unconscious for the world, a deep control beneath the oceans and continents'.

This is the kind of presence which, in almost all other cities, has long since been built over, obscured. But it is this geology in which the city is so nakedly rooted which is also at the basis of Cape Town's attractive power – the immense, almost gravitational force its setting exerts. It is a city whose mystique lies, above all, in its physique. It is the sheer physicality of the place that is both most immediate and long-lasting in its hold.

One feels it not only in the rock and stone that add their strata, literally, to one's daily life. One knows it throughout every summer, when the peninsula is ransacked by the trades blowing in from the south-east ocean. It is driven home, come winter, in those fronts which, originating in bursts of cold air from Antarctica, overrun the peninsula in an arc of rain-bearing cloud that can curve away, such is the force gathered in them, almost as far as South America. It is these elements, severally or together, which make for a singular kind of addiction. Citizens of Cape Town grow up, like few others on earth, knowing what the American poet Wallace Stevens was trying to suggest when he wrote his famous line: 'The greatest poverty is not to live in a physical world.'

They know something else besides. This is the further wealth of being able to inhabit a city which effortlessly reverses that which cities generically declare: the defeat of the natural world and the absolute pre-eminence of human beings; of culture over nature. Overwhelmed by the presence of its mountains, its own urban reaches diminished by the expanse of sea around it, and all of it overarched by enormous sky, Cape Town inverts the usual relation between the built environment and the environs that the natural world has built. It continues to offer something which almost all other cities in the twenty-first century have lost – a home in which human beings do not have to suffer the exile of being a species so dominant that they have obliterated all but the signs, the scars, of their own presence. Even in the midst of its downtown streets, the stone world has not yet become completely other.

Nor – still more addictively – has the green world become other here.

There is in fact a kingdom at the end of more than one of those same streets; or not that far beyond. This is the realm created by the fynbos biome, the Cape Floral Kingdom, one of the world's six and, for its size, the richest in species. It establishes that place apart, yet seen so readily within the city, which enables us to be witnesses, again on an almost daily basis, to an ideal city even while we are immured in the toils of the real one.

Perhaps there are the glimmerings, always, of such a place in whatever city – moments when a beauty struggles through the urban decay, the grimness of weather, to shine forth. But here in Cape Town, these are more than glimmerings. It is hardly fanciful to say that a paradise lies within easy walking distance of the city centre. And though Capetonians might know that paradise is never where human beings actually live (it is invariably what they have left or lost), it reappears each day along the mountain's upper slopes, among its ericas and restios. The citizens of this city, in short, are accompanied, in their exile in the urban world, by an anti-world, the shadow of a realm that is neither distant nor fallen – or not yet.

It is built not only by those thousands of wild flowers and reed grasses, by sky and weather, but also by a certain quality of light. It is a light which, on certain days, can come to seem in itself a spiritual condition. It is one which, appearing most often after a north-west front has passed over the peninsula, builds us its own world, re-imagining this city, painting it as it might have been – or perhaps still could be. In its long focus – such is its power to clarify – things once again come to have all the reality they can have.

Having once experienced it, you will want always to see this light again. And seeing it again, you will find yourself as often regretting, long in advance (you hope), the day you will have to die. You will know what Kipling meant when years ago, writing of this same light at the Cape, he spoke of it as having 'bound tight chains' around his heart, and the hearts of those in his family, for many years to come. And you will understand better why it is that those who left this city are not simply afflicted by homesickness. In consequence of their loss – such is the nature of Cape Town – they are brought very close at times to appreciating what the psychologists mean when they say that, at root, all human beings are both insatiable and inconsolable.

III

There is no doubt that those who have never left Cape Town can be no less afflicted by such things as its light, their feeling for it no less sure to bind strong chains around their hearts.

'Stupendous, miserable city' – such were the terms in which Pier Paolo Pasolini, the Italian writer, was once moved to invoke Rome, the city of his maturity. And few among those who have continued to live in Cape Town have not been similarly provoked. That it is – and always was – stupendous, every breaking day confirms. That it was also home to a bleakness that goes beyond even the more desolating reaches of that word – this is no less patent.

It can, in fact, be a city of unrivalled melancholy. It always was. In part this melancholy has its origins in the city's beginnings as a way-station – that place, nothing in itself, to which people go only to get to somewhere else. In part it has to do with its location, on the bottommost rim of Africa, on that edge of emptiness multiplied to infinity which is the south Atlantic. It lies also, bewilderingly, in the flip side to that aspect of the city which I have just praised: the ease with which the city's built environment is swallowed up and otherwise dwarfed by the huge, vacant spaces of the Cape sky. And it persists in the southeaster always blowing – so it sometimes seems – and blowing to no end.

It is one of the world's great depressive winds, so like that illness in its total, pointed vehemence; and like depression, too, in its total, vehement aimlessness. Under its onslaught each summer, all of Cape Town loses its anchorage and becomes a place as unfinished as it ever was in its colonial beginnings, fraying into emptiness, the roads drifted in sand, the wattle flannelled in dust, the buildings floating in space, disconnected one from another. It becomes a city both lonely in space and time – and almost unique in its power to afflict its citizens with a homesickness even while they continue to live there.

In this respect it is not simply like other cities – Pasolini's Rome again, where, as he writes in his *Stories from the City of God* (2003), 'beauty and ugliness go hand in hand' and where, better still, 'the latter renders the former touching and human' while 'the former allows us to forget the latter'. It is a place, rather, which would seem to offer, again and again, the widest possible discrepancy between the works of God and the desecrations of man – and, at the same time, the shortest possible distance between the two.

This was most obviously so in earlier decades. Apartheid not only emptied the city of certain population groups; it emptied it of life. Then the brutalities visited on the city were only augmented by the boredoms that all tyrannies enforce. And it was then, too, that the contraries of the place were at their most bewildering, ensnaring.

On the one hand there was the beauty that it continued to possess and that stood there, with all the self-evidence that beauty possesses, irrefutably. On the other, in a contradiction that was as unrelieved as it was bitter, there reigned the cruel and foolish designs of politics, and poverty, depravity. It is under the sign of this contradiction that Cape Town has perhaps always existed. But it was as the very archetype of the ruined paradise – the place that promises everything and yet delivers very little – that it existed at that time. And we who went on living there could scarcely escape living under the same sign as well. We could not shake off the extraordinary power of the place to generate an intense ambivalence of feeling towards it.

Love-hate relationships, though they can be as compelling and entrapping as any other, are also, finally, wearying. One grows tired of a love that is repeatedly contaminated by anger and sorrow and pity. There were times – too many – in my own Cape Town past when I simply wanted to do what so many others had done before me: to get out of the place. What held me back, perhaps, was nothing more or less than that which kept a similar, much discouraged character, as described in Philip Roth's *Sabbath's Theatre* (1995), rooted to his spot: 'How could he leave? Everything he hated was here.'

IV

A person writes so much about a place not because he belongs, but because he wants to belong. He writes about a city, seeking out its hidden coordinates, the substructures that might define it – the character of its light, the dryness of its stone – not only because he knows instinctively, as the American writer Flannery O'Connor once put it, that 'if you are going to write you'd better have somewhere to come from'.

In fact I did not understand, in my youth, that in writing

about Cape Town I was trying to compensate for the degree to which that city, like the rest of South Africa at the time, afflicted me with a sense of homelessness. My passionate identification with the place was fuelled by a no less impassioned sense of homelessness. The stone of its streets, the sight of the sea and its confluence with sky, whether drained of light or light-filled, the precise way in which it bleached with the onset of the first winds of summer – I tried for a long time to invest such things with all that I lacked, all that was lost, and which indeed could not be found. I was one of those who write about a city, peopling it, but also trying to capture that meeting of coastline and skyline – those impalpable things – in order to define and create a home for himself, a home that does not exist – and then, beyond that, to reinvent for himself, in his own exile, a lost kingdom, the lost tradition.

Now it is a long time after.

From year to year, and ever more rapidly lately, one notices the changes that have come about: the villas of the *arrivistes*, still rose and vanilla, that keep on going up, the division and subdivision of old properties to make way for townhouses, the new office blocks, convention centres, and those emptinesses without a centre, the giant shopping malls. Millions of rand in foreign investment are pouring into the city – one reads this daily in the papers. Slowly at first, but more and more quickly now – the way they say people go bankrupt – the city is losing its own past, as if already it had lost its shadow.

But if you live long enough in one environment, there is another sort of change that comes about, albeit more slowly. There is a sense in which, in time, you come into possession of a place, even if this has little to do with whether you own property there or are a member of the political or social elite. It happens because of a certain alteration in feeling that the Greek Alexandrian Cavafy, perhaps the greatest of the city poets in the past century, captures in one of his very brief, late poems before his death in 1933.

In the Same Space

The setting of houses, cafés, the neighbourhood
that I've seen and walked through years on end:

I created you while I was happy, while I was sad,
with so many incidents, so many details.

And, for me, the whole of you has been transformed into
    feeling.

Cavafy knew that, in time, all features of a place, even the more repellent, are subsumed by something else. One recognises, more and more, the full force of that verb 'to recognise'. To know again what one has known before, to see not new things but old things seen anew – this, though it may not be the most profound experience open to a human being, is one of the great privileges of having lived in one city for many years.

These can be the most ordinary, even commonplace things. In fact, it is better if they are so. I, for one, never fail to notice how, in Cape Town, towards the end of February each year, the nightly dewfalls begin to thicken, the grass is dulled by cold each morning. The days of March – of thin, dry heat – return. It's the time of year when, the year itself beginning to turn, you wait for the morning when, for the first time in months, you can see on the far arm of the bay the stone of the mountains softened by cloud-shadow, the slopes, usually hazed by wind, brought into focus by the darkness those shadows take on in the suddenly cooler, pre-autumn air. It is the first of signs by which we know that summer is really over.

Others might notice other things: the look of the fynbos, and the calmness that inhabits it, up on the eastern flanks of the mountain, after rain. But these are the pleasures that, as they recur each year, help one to understand why human beings should attach so much importance to place, why they should grow so *attached*. They underline why it is that the word 'home' is freighted with as many connotations as any in the language; and why its polar opposite, exile, has always been regarded as perhaps the most bitter of the deprivations a human being can be forced to suffer. And they make one wonder afresh what it must be like to live in an environment and not to find in it, its weather or streets, those familiar things that make us less unfamiliar to ourselves.

V

Perhaps this is also why, in my mind, more and more another city supervenes, taking precedence over all others.

I know that Cape Town will continue, for decades hence, to bear the disfigurements of the apartheid city it once was. The fearful disaster perpetrated by certain of its town planners – most notably the Foreshore's raised highway that has erected a cordon sanitaire between the city and the sea – will not be breached for a long time. The Flats will continue to flood in winter, the droughts to starve the region of water as global warming pushes the rain-bearing fronts far south of the peninsula. Metropolitan politics will doubtless persist, here as elsewhere in South Africa, as the public domain (though lately privatised) of the seven deadly sins, avarice chief amongst them.

On any morning, years hence, there will be the sight,

soon after daybreak, of people sheltering in the doorways of locked shops, sunning themselves out of the wind after a night sleeping rough, out on the slopes of the mountain. More and more one anticipates a new form of enclosure in this city, whole tracts of land carved out of the peninsula for those latter-day concentration camps for the rich, the walled and gated golfing estates. One can even foresee a time when the mountain, so far from dominating the city, will assume more the character of a periscope, its summit plateau hardly able to rise above an ocean of stalled, polluted air.

All this will persist; and with it that edge of desolation. Yet it is another city that keeps surfacing – and resurfacing. This is, after all, the place to which foreigners and others, in their thousands, have lately come. They have moved here, the German couple who once chanced to stop off en route to Australia and who knew at once they needed to go no further; the Canadians tired only of Regina, Saskatchewan (as they were to discover) and not of life; the refugees who have escaped from various states in central Africa; and not least those countless others who have defected from villages in the interior.

Behind them lies the perfect, dull upholstery of their years in certain welfare states; the long grind, perhaps, of those Canadian winters that, though Canadian-born, they never got used to; things unspeakable in the Democratic Republic of the Congo; or, more simply, beginnings in small towns in the hinterland that always seemed to those born there more accidental, even, than the accident of their birth.

Before them lies something – a prospect – that can still be seen, and which can still take the native-born Capetonian by surprise. You can chance upon it even in the morning gridlocks that now choke, as they will in the future, Cape Town's roads. It can happen to each and all of us – the housewives, lives marooned between the washing and the carpool, the clerical official preparing for another day of exile, in administration, from his better self, true life. It can be granted no less to those, always with us now, armoured in those monuments to conspicuous, careless consumption, their 4x4s.

Preoccupied, unaware – like them, you look up. An ordinary morning, midweek, the mountain long since at work, spinning its daily cloud off the sea wind. But you see a city in the hem of that mountain, the sea that parented it. It is a place that, even as it materialises, is dematerialising – the mountain losing a hold on its own skyline, thinning in the cloud now blowing off it, its sandstone by now no more than a version of cloud.

And you feel something that, though it's similar – very nearly immaterial – is only so because it is without price. You feel how you are part of this, are being gathered into it; how in this city, shaped by its wind, you are being woven once more into the fabric of a further day. And for a moment you're surprised – because you've lived here for many years, you've seen this many times before, and you hardly expect by now to be visited here, in the stalled, Cape Town traffic, by that oldest of afflictions this city can induce: this longing, once again, to say unforgettable things.

Stephen Watson has published five volumes of poetry, including The Other City: Selected Poems (2000), Selected Essays (1990) and A Writer's Diary (1997), as well as having edited several other books, most recently Dante in South Africa (2005).